D0242294

Jacob's War

Jacob's War

By

Robert John Bullock

Strategic Book Publishing and Rights Co.

Copyright © 2013 Robert John Bullock. All rights reserved.

No part of this book may be reproduced or transmitted in any form or by any means, graphic, electronic, or mechanical, including photocopying, recording, taping, or by any information storage retrieval system, without the permission, in writing, of the publisher.

Strategic Book Publishing and Rights Co.
12620 FM 1960, Suite A4-507
Houston TX 77065
www.sbpra.com

ISBN: 978-1-62212-582-1

CONTENTS

ACKNOWLEDGEMENTS & DEDICATIONS

This book is dedicated to all the people interned under Regulation 18B, many of them innocent men, women and children who were opposed to Hitler's government, many of them persecuted by the Nazi's, many of them refugees who had sought refuge in Great Britain.

Alien internment is often seen, quite rightly, as one of Britain's darkest hours, but when you put it in the context of the pressure of war with Germany you can start to understand why it happened. By undertaking the research for this book I can now understand a little of how people must have felt in 1940, how my grandparents, aunts and uncles must have felt. In 1940 fear of invasion by German was a very real and present prospect and the British people were terrified.

The Isle of Man wasn't the only place that aliens were taken, there were many camps on the main land, especially in the North West of England. But there wasn't anywhere else quite like the Rushen Camp.

Dame Joanna Cruikshank was indeed a real person who had a distinguished, long and successful career.

The stories of German ladies sunbathing and swimming in the sea naked are real, it did really happen, as was the subsequent outrage!

The despicable sinking of the Arandora Star really happened at the hands of Günter Prien and U-47, and hundreds died in the icy Atlantic waters. Prien who was awarded the Knight's Cross of the Iron Cross with Oak Leaves (Germany's highest military decoration at the time) and his crew lurked beneath the ocean sank a total of 30 commercial ships and one warship, as well as damaging a further eight commercial ships and a warship before he was reported missing, assumed dead in Spring 1941, though there is no official record of what happened to U-47, Prien and his 44 crewmen. But such was the reputation of Günter Prien that his death was announced to the House of Commons by Winston Churchill himself!

From my research I understand that the summer of 1940 was indeed one of the best summers ever for weather for the Isle of Man! Perfect for sunbathing and swimming in the sea!

I am indebted to all the people I have corresponded with and spoken to whilst researching this book. Although 1940 seems like a lifetime ago to me I feel honoured that I have been able to speak with people who, like Jacob, Terry, Sarah and Laila, were children in internment camps on the Isle of Man. My thanks go out to them for sharing their memories with me. I hope I have done justice to their experiences and memories.

I would like to thank everyone at the Manx National Library Archive in Douglas, their expertise and patience was vital in helping me unlock and understand the story of internment on the island. I could not have done it without them.

I would sincerely like to thank Arts Council England for generously supporting my research for this novel. Their vital support allowed me to visit the Isle of Man, and museums and archives across the country. But even more than this was the fact that this project was worthy of the support of such an esteemed organisation. This meant such a lot to a budding writer like me.

As ever, I would like to thank my family and friends for all their support.

Last, but not least, I would like to thank my beautiful, ever patient wife, Kristen, for helping get the project off the ground, get it up and running and hardest of all, get it completed! She has been there every step of the way and has always been the best support team anyone could have.

R J Bullock Oct 2012

Prologue

THE HOUSE OF COMMONS, LONDON JANUARY 1940

It was a dark, damp and rainy January morning when, just before lunch-time, the freedom of many British men, women and children was to be snatched away from them in the name of liberty and freedom.

Readying himself, the Edinburgh born Home Secretary, Sir John Anderson, took a deep breath, stood up and cleared his throat as the throng of excitement died down just enough for him to make one of the most important announcements of the Second World War.

"I announce to this House today," declared Anderson, grimly but clearly, "that under Regulation 18B, I make an order that all people of German and Italian descent be detained indefinitely in camps until the threat that they pose to our country be clearly determined."

Chapter 1

RUN!

Jacob Becker's arms ached, his muscles and sinews strained as he pumped them vigorously. It was as if he were punching his worst enemy with all the strength in his young body. *Punch! Punch! Punch!* A blow to the body! An upper cut to the chin! A crunching left jab in the face! *Punch! Punch!* He hit out as hard as he could, his Boston Red Sox jacket flapping wildly about his chest relying only on his thin red t-shirt and denim jeans to keep the cold wind from his body. There was no way he could stop. The next blow could be his very last.

Oh how Jacob wished he could batter those responsible for this terrible nightmare!

His young body was draining every last ounce of effort from his muscles and lungs even though they were screaming and screaming for it to stop. But Jacob could not stop or the enemy would capture him.

He sprinted hard pounding the concrete, his new sneakers gripping the wet quayside with each bounding stride, but the men were starting to close in on him. Jacob was athletic but there were at least a dozen of them and they had cars and motorbikes while he had just his legs.

As the dusk started creeping along the dockside, Jacob's mind started wandering. *Why me, God?* He thought, his mind drifting into a trance to try to block out the pain and fear. *Why do bad things happen to me and my family? Why, God? We've never even hurt a fly! Why are they trying to do this to me? They've already got Sarah, Mum, Dad and Gran, and now I'm the only one left for them to round up like an animal! Don't they have enough to do fighting Hitler and his armies? Do they really have to pick on twelve year old kids?*

"Don't you have enough to do, fighting Hitler?" he shouted back angrily at the chasers, his thick blond hair falling across his eyes as he turned. The words just slipped out, an extension of his thoughts.

"Cheeky little beggar!" cursed one man, though in reality Jacob wasn't little at all, he was almost six feet tall and looked at least sixteen.

"Stop right now!" shouted another, "you're making things a lot worse for yourself, lad!"

"Worse?" shouted Jacob, half laughing, though he was panting so deeply he could barely get the words out of his mouth, "how?"

How could things get any worse? How?

Jacob had easily broken free from his captors. He was a strong boy who boxed, played football, ice hockey and was a black belt at Judo. He was easily more than a match for a couple of stupid, old guards who looked like somebody's wrinkled grandads.

He had slipped from their grasp and kicked the rear doors of the rickety van open as they drove him to the monstrous prisoner ship. The other two boys in the van were too scared to go with Jacob as he yelled at them to follow him, so he set off alone. Jacob was an independent boy so this wasn't anything new to him. He wasn't afraid, if no one would come with him, he'd go it alone!

Although he used to live in Liverpool, Jacob Becker had been a young child, just five, when he left. Yet his father had often described the docks by the side of the bustling River Mersey, which had been one of the world's busiest shipping ports for almost two hundred years, so he felt like he knew it well. He felt as if his knowledge gave him home field advantage.

As the gasping guards called after him, Jacob pumped his arms harder still and accelerated away from them, passing the famous landmarks of the dockside. He passed the Royal Liver Building with its famous stone Liver Birds perched on top watching everything below them with little more than a modicum of interest. He ran passed the Port of Liverpool Building that controlled so much of the shipping that entered and left the city. And finally he passed the immense Cunard Building, which housed the shipping company famous for ships like the Queen Mary, the Queen Elizabeth and even the Titanic, when the company was called the White Star Line.

Jacob hated that company so much. They were responsible for Grandad Becker's death twenty five years ago because they were the ones that had built that stupid ship, the Lusitania. Oh how he hated that ship! That ship had been the reason his grandfather had been killed and why his dad had got into so much trouble with the government.

"I hate that stupid ship!" he yelled.

Jacob leapt over a couple of iron bollards and moved to dodge some drunken sailors who were making the most of their shore leave.

"Oy!" shouted one of them, "Watch it, lad!"

"Yeah, watch it!" mimicked his stumbling mate.

"Stop him!" called the guards at the sailors as they staggered after the boy.

The men, slow to realise what was happening, lunged forward and tried to block Jacob's path but he just lowered his shoulder and scuttled the men as if he were playing a game of ten pin bowls.

On and on Jacob ran. He had no idea where he was going but he sure knew it wasn't going to be on to that death ship and to the prisoner of war camp on that island in the middle of nowhere.

THUD!!

"Ow!!" Jacob's head snapped forward.

Something heavy caught Jacob on the back of the head, making his knees buckle beneath him like a cartoon character at the end of a comic chase scene. In slow motion, Jacob started to black out as he crashed to the ground. The last thing Jacob remembered before finally losing consciousness was a stern, fat faced policeman standing over him, sheathing his big, black wooden truncheon with one hand whilst catching him with the other.

"Allo, allo, allo! Now then young fella me lad! What's all this about then?" asked the policeman as Jacob started to black out.

"Th..th..they're taking me... prisoner...not German...I'm Am...Am...Americ...American..." stuttered Jacob as he blacked out.

Chapter 2

THE DAY BEFORE YESTERDAY

"I don't know why we had to come back at all," moaned Jacob Becker's pretty blonde mum, Elisabeth, as the Becker family sat around Grossmutter, or Grandmother, Geli Becker's large kitchen table in Balham, south west London, eating a traditional German breakfast.

Although Carl and Elisabeth Becker were enjoying being with Geli again, they hadn't wanted to leave their comfortable life in the USA for war torn London and their children, Jacob and Sarah would certainly rather have been back home in Concord, Massachusetts.

"Well, to be really honest, Elisabeth," replied Carl Becker taking a piece of Weißwurst, or white sausage, adding it to a plate that was already well stacked with a selection of breads, cheeses and pretzels, "Jim did say that Bawdsey Manor asked for me personally you know, work of the gravest national importance he said."

"Work of the gravest national importance!" Elizabeth snorted.

"...reading between the lines I don't think I had much of a choice, honey."

"Choice! You're an American citizen now, Carl, of course you had a choice!" snapped Elisabeth, "and Geli could have come over to us, we could have organised something, what has she got keeping her here?"

"Oy! I have friends here!" protested a hurt looking Geli, "you know zat."

"Electronic communications is quite a close community, honey..." continued Carl ignoring his mother, "everyone knows everyone else's business, Bawdsey Manor said I was the man for the job, work of the gravest..."

"DON'T say that again!" Elizabeth pointed at her husband with a butter knife.

"Oh...and MIT agreed. Err..." Carl peered over at the stove, "is there any more coffee going, Mutti?"

MIT or the Massachusetts Institute of Technology was a leading private research university located in Cambridge, Massachusetts, USA. Seven years earlier in June 1933 the university had head hunted Professor Carl Becker for a secret research position within the university, he was to join a small established team working on electronic communication and the development of a new early warning system known as Radar (radio detection and ranging). Over the past seven years Carl had been back to the UK many times to work with colleagues from Bawdsey, who were conducting ground breaking research. Yet most of his actual research had been in the United States.

So with the selfless blessing of the Becker family matriarch, Geli, Carl Becker, his wife Elisabeth, his five year old son Jacob and three year old daughter Sarah had left their Liverpool home in the north west of England for a new life in the United States.

And the Becker children, especially, had really taken to the American way of life, like ducks to water. In reality, ten year old Sarah had virtually no recollection of life in Liverpool and she only knew England from the family's visits to see Grossmutti in London every two years. Even Jacob only remembered snippets from life before moving to the States. To them, Jacob and Sarah, the Becker family were, to all intents and purposes, American. They did not want to return to England, especially with a war raging in Europe, no matter what the reason.

However, Carl Becker was English born and he was a patriot, the phrase 'gravest national importance' really meant something to him. He hadn't told his family but his chief at MIT, Professor

Stanley Geller had in fact given him a choice when the British research team leader, Professor Jim Wilson had approached him asking for Becker to return to work on a new project. Yet Carl had said he didn't have a choice to make, he had to return, he had to be part of the war effort and the development of this technology, especially with America sitting on the fence about joining the war.

Geli nearly jumped out of her skin as the phone in the parlour started ringing.

"It's just the telephone, Mutti," Carl jumped to his feet. To the American Beckers, telephones were very much part of their daily lives, but to Geli it was still a novelty because it had only just been installed by the War Department so they could get in touch with Carl easily.

Two minutes after disappearing, Carl reappeared through the kitchen door, grabbed a piece of bread, smeared it with butter, pulled his jacket on and hastily gulped the last of his coffee, before picking up his trilby hat and popping it on to his head.

"I've got to go out," he mumbled with his mouth full.

"Where to, Carl?" questioned Elisabeth.

"Aw, you know I can't say, honey!" sighed Carl, "gravest..."

"Carl!"

"Mmm...shouldn't be long though. Oh yeah, before I forget, you're all going to be moved to the safety of the countryside soon! Wiltshire I think they said."

"What?" Elisabeth stared at Carl.

Carl ignored her and continued, "so it would be kind of a good idea to start packing a few things today cos we'll be going tomorrow, see ya!"

"What?" called Elisabeth after him, "What? What did you say, Carl! CARL!"

"Carl!" called Geli as well, "What are you talking about, Carl?" but the door slammed shut and Carl was gone.

Chapter 3

TERRY LOWE

Much, much too worse for wear, dark haired, swarthy skinned sixteen year old Terry Lowe from Yorkshire crouched down low on the damp Liverpool dockside.

Terry had been drinking far too much beer and at this precise moment in time, through his blurry 'beer goggles' he was super human and almost anything was possible to him. Terry was on the lookout for a ship to take him to America and freedom from imprisonment.

He'd spent all the previous night asking around in almost all the dockland bars that were filled with seamen from around the world but everyone was curiously tight lipped and no one would help him. But he had been clumsy and had attracted the attention of the intelligence service, which had eyes and ears everywhere. Taking the bull by the horns, the impetuous young Terry had decided he didn't need anyone's help and he planned to pinch the first boat he came across on the dockside.

That first boat that Terry spotted was the Emma Dee, a small chubby tugboat from North Wales, which was used to help the larger ships negotiate the difficult currents of the River Mersey before being towed into the Irish Sea.

Terry Lowe had never been on a sea-going boat before, the closest he had come to a maritime adventure was when his family had visited Lake Windermere, in the English Lake District, and taken a steamer from Bowness to Ambleside, just a few miles along the lake!

Terry was an apprentice cobbler from Skipton, in the Yorkshire Dales. The son of a Jewish master cobbler originally from Dresden, Germany, young Terry had been arrested as part of the new British policy of sending anybody with any links with Germany to prison, regardless of their professions, history, religion or sex. As in the Great War, most of the prisoners were being shipped over to the Isle of Man, a small island in the middle of the Irish Sea where they would be out of sight and out of mind.

Terry was so drunk, however, that he didn't see the policemen watching him approach the Emma Dee. And he definitely didn't hear them sniggering as he lost his footing on the dockside, scrambled to stay out of the murky water and then fell clumsily on to the old tugboat.

"Ow!" he grumbled to himself as he rubbed his sore head, "now where's that steering wheel at?"

Terry fumbled around the dark boat until he eventually found the main cabin of the fat little boat.

Thud!! Thud!! Thud!! Heavy men in boots were landing on the deck, yet Terry was too engrossed in figuring out Emma's layout to be concerned.

"Ah! Got it!" mumbled a triumphant Terry, starting the engine.

Much to his surprise, the Emma Dee roared to life, and not bothering to untie the boat, Terry turned the ship's wheel and opened the throttle fully!

"Oy!" somebody yelled from behind Terry's back, grabbing the lever and closing the throttle down.

"What?" Terry spun around and lost his footing again, slipped and banged his head hard. Trying to steady himself, his hand grabbed at the first thing it came across, the throttle lever again, and he accidentally pushed it forward once more.

This time Emma lurched powerfully from the dockside, taking some of her moorings with her, and surged out to the centre of the river.

As Terry was passing out he could just hear the policemen arguing about what to do to get back to shore.

"What do I do?" called one.

"I don't know, do I look like a sailor!" argued another, "Jim, Jim, what do we do?"

"How should I know what to do?" Jim's panic stricken face clearly indicating his lack of sailing knowledge!

Those were the last words Terry heard, he didn't remember anything else.

Chapter 4

CARL BECKER DISCOVERS HIS
FAMILY ARE MISSING

The house was deathly silent as he opened the front door. Carl Becker had been at the Ministry of War much longer than he thought he would be. In fact he was there for almost twenty four hours in total. Carl often became so engrossed in his work that he forgot what time it was. He'd often forget to eat or drink as well as sleep. Elisabeth was always telling him off for not taking enough care of himself.

It was just a few minutes after nine o'clock before he carefully pushed his key in the lock of Geli's door and slowly pushed it open.

Got to be quiet as a mouse, he thought. Perhaps if he sneaked in and went straight upstairs he could pretend he'd been back all night? Maybe nobody would be any the wiser!

Yet as soon as he entered the house everything felt strangely wrong. The atmosphere felt different. There was no sound at all coming from the normally bustling home and with two children, a bossy wife and a nosey mother this wasn't right at all. There was just the sound of Mutti's grandmother clock in the parlour, rhythmically ticking away the hours, minutes and seconds of the day, just like it did every day. That clock was the sound of Carl's childhood, it was almost the first thing he remembered from being a really small child, the ticking and the chiming, day and night, winter, summer, spring and autumn. Birthdays and celebrations came and went, the clock ticking away in the background. Now the sound of the clock was the only noise in the entire house.

"Hello!" called Carl, any idea of trying to creep in now completely gone from his head.

There was no response.

"Hello!" he called again, "Anyone home?"

Nothing.

That's funny! he thought, *They should be in. We've got to leave today.*

Carl noticed a note left under the black bakelite telephone on the small table just in front of him.

"Uh? What's this?" he muttered, picking up the note and quickly unfolding it.

"Carl, I called the all the numbers you left for me but no one could find you anywhere!" wrote Elisabeth, "It's unbelievable! The most dreadful thing is happening. Shortly after you left for work the police arrived at our door, a man and a woman. They knocked loudly and when I answered they said they had come to take us to prison..."

"To prison?" Carl couldn't believe what he was reading, "To prison?" he repeated out loud.

"...yes prison. We are to be taken to the Isle of Man, you remember we visited it once when we lived in Liverpool?"

"I remember," answered Carl though he knew no one could hear him, "it rained all the time we were there."

"It rained all the time we were there!"

"I remember!" muttered the scientist.

"They said they were taking us because we are German..." continued Elisabeth.

"We're NOT German. We're Americans now!" shouted Carl, "English by birth but naturalised Americans!"

"I told them we were American citizens, English by birth but now Americans, naturalised Americans, I even showed them our passports, but they said they had orders to take anyone with any links to Germany!"

"Did they mistreat you?" asked Carl though he knew Elisabeth couldn't hear him.

"They are treating us very fairly though," replied Elisabeth, "in fact they are being very nice about it..."

"Well that's good of them!" spat Carl angrily.

"...and they even made tea and toast whilst we packed to keep us going for the long journey. It not their fault, Carl, they are only doing their jobs."

"Doing their jobs?" Carl was furious.

"Carl, you've got to do something, this is a big mistake, a terrible mistake. Come and get us and then we can all go back to Concord, Geli too. Do something quick, Carl! Please! Your loving wife, Elisabeth xxx."

"What can I do?" said Carl out loud, anxiously running his fingers through his thick, blond hair.

Thinking quickly he picked up the phone and called the Ministry of War.

"Hello, Ministry of War," answered the female telephonist efficiently, "who do you require?"

"This is Professor Carl Becker, I want to speak with someone about my wife!" Carl was angry and not thinking clearly'.

"I'm sorry, Sir," replied the woman politely, "but I don't understand."

"My wife and children and mother have been arrested!"

"I am so sorry, Sir, but that sounds like a matter for the police, perhaps you would like to hang up and redial New Scotland Yard, the number is..."

"I don't want the number for New Scotland Yard!" yelled Carl, cutting the telephonist short, "they've been arrested because we're a German family!"

Chapter 5

LAILA LEVY

Fresh faced, with long dark brown hair, green eyes and a rosy complexion, Laila Levy looked every inch the perfect English rose. She spoke beautiful English with not a trace of a foreign accent, was doing very well at school, had lots of good friends and was even learning to play the viola. But Laila wasn't English at all, she was German, German born and bred. She didn't have any family in England and hadn't heard for the past ten months whether her family back in Berlin were even alive. Laila Levy was a German Jewish refugee who had escaped from Berlin on the Kinderstransport with thousands of other children and had sought sanctuary in England.

Although she had been in England for almost ten months and had in many ways settled in really well, Laila Levy sometimes still felt she was a stranger in a strange land. She always felt lonely and worried about her family and friends back home, especially in the quiet darkness of her small bedroom in the middle of the night.

When she first arrived in London she could speak only a few words of English. 'Yes', 'no', 'please' and 'thank you' were drummed into her relentlessly by her parents in the few weeks before she left Germany so she wouldn't appear rude, but still she felt like she'd arrived on the moon when her train slowly pulled into Waterloo Station on the 21st June 1939. She had no brothers or sisters or friends or family members with her to share the experience. Laila was completely alone.

The Kindertransport, also known as the Refugee Children Movement, was a children's rescue mission that took place nine months prior to the outbreak of World War II and moved thousands and thousands of children from Germany and other parts of war torn Europe to safety in Great Britain.

Laila's family were devout Jews and since Adolf Hitler's Nationalist Socialist Party had come to power in Germany they had constantly threatened Jewish people and those of other religions. So, as a last resort, many parents like Laila's had made the heartbreaking decision that the tolerant United Kingdom was the safest place for their precious children.

Unlike many, the Levy family, although having no relatives residing in London were able to make provision for their daughter. Laila had been met at Waterloo by a Mrs Freidrich, who was a German friend of a friend of the Levy family. She wasn't Jewish and she didn't have a husband because he had left her many years before for a younger, prettier woman, and she was also quite poor. When Laila's family, who were rich, and were from an old established family of bankers in Berlin, had asked Mrs Freidrich to look after their daughter for a generous regular monthly allowance she had jumped at the chance to give up her boring work in a sweaty little office in the city of London and sit about all day doing absolutely nothing!

Laila had quickly discovered that Mrs Freidrich particularly enjoyed doing nothing, she laid in bed each day until noon, invariably didn't get dressed beyond pulling on her moth eaten old dressing gown and pink fluffy slippers and never, ever, did a stroke of housework. "Housework is for the working class, dear!" she used to tell Laila, who was forced to clean, cook and wash for her. As for Mrs Freidrich, she was definitely not working class, she was upper middle class! And she told Laila over and over again that the upper middle class had servants. Laila quickly realised that *she* was in fact Mrs Freidrich's servant!

Apart from the endless housework, life at Mrs Freidrich's terraced house at 37 Durley Road in Amhurst Park, North

London was boring for the then seven year old Laila, and even now wasn't much better. There were no other children in the house, few children in the neighbourhood, and hardly anybody ever called. Mrs Freidrich just spent her days and evenings smoking foul smelling cigarettes and drinking gin which she got from the only person who ever called at the house, a spiv called Mr Bannister, Oliver Bannister, a man with a moustache that looked like a worm! The rest of Mrs Freidrich's days were spent reading old German books.

Laughter and frivolity were completely and utterly "Verboten!" or forbidden at 37 Durley Road, and German was the only language spoken. As a consequence of this Laila always looked forward to the weekdays that she spent at the local primary school.

School was difficult to begin with, all the lessons were different from back in Germany and she didn't understand anyone except a couple of German boys, who had arrived on the same Kinderstransport as her. These boys were so horribly rude to her all the time that the only option for Laila was to learn English as quickly as possible and make some new English friends!

When Laila first arrived, her parents were due to come over to England to join her within weeks and Mutti had written after just a couple of days to say they were organising their papers so they could come very soon. That one solitary letter had been the only contact that Laila had had with her parents in the last ten months. Naturally, she was distraught by this but Mrs Freidrich seemed quite happy because each and every month without fail her money arrived, she'd even got a raise at the start of the year, and so she was able to keep her cigarette and gin supply from Mr Oliver Bannister open and flowing freely.

Then, one morning everything was turned on its head. When the policeman and woman had arrived at the house and banged on the door, Laila thought at first that they had come to tell them some bad news about her parents, that they'd been hurt or worse, killed by Hitler's Nazis. But when they said they had come to take them both away her fears turned to the possibility that they might be sending them both back to Germany because of the war, or maybe because of their relationship with Mr Oliver Bannister, who Laila had always thought looked shifty. She thought that people with worm moustaches always looked shifty.

During the journey to Euston Station in a black taxi, Laila had decided suddenly that she hated Germans so much she would never speak their dreadful language ever again! Ever! If someone spoke to her in German she would answer in English, and as an added bonus this would annoy Mrs Freidrich! Annoying Mrs Freidrich could be good fun! There and then Laila decided that everything was all the fault of the Germans! Them, their strange language and that funny little man with an even stranger looking moustache than Mr Oliver Bannister's!

Chapter 6

THE HOLDING STATION

Like Laila Levy, the Becker ladies also travelled from London's Euston station north on England's west coast railway line to the town of Wigan, in Lancashire, where they waited for what seemed like hours and hours before getting on another train and travelling on to the city of Liverpool.

Of course, it was all quite familiar to Elisabeth Becker who used to live near Liverpool and on the way she pointed out lots of landmarks to her daughter and told her the history of some of the towns and cities that Sarah had only heard about.

More than nine hours after leaving home the train finally pulled into the station at the famous sea port of Liverpool. Everyone alighted and made their way to a big old warehouse building near the dockside. There they sat in a huge old hall along with hundreds and hundreds of other distressed women and children but not a single man. Nobody seemed to know exactly what was happening just that they were being taken to 'that island' to be thrown into dark, damp and cold prisons.

"Oh, I'm sure it won't be *that* bad," Elisabeth tried to reassure her daughter and cheer her up, she nodded and winked at Geli to join in.

"No, no," Geli shook her head, understanding straight away that her daughter-in-law was trying to keep Sarah happy, "I have heard that it is quite a nice place to visit."

"Yeah! They've got lots of nice sandy beaches, lovely cafes and cats without tails," Elisabeth's jolly tone caught Sarah's attention.

"Cats *without* tails?" asked Sarah, "but, Mom, all cats have got tails, it helps them balance when they jump from tree to tree!"

"Not Manx cats, Sarah," assured Elisabeth, "they have no tails at all."

"No way, Mom! I don't believe it," Sarah was adamant.

"Ah," spoke a strange voice, butting in, "I zink some of zem do actually have a leettle stumpy tail," it was a very wrinkled grey haired old lady that butted in. She was sitting in the seat next to Geli.

"Do they?" asked Elisabeth, "I thought that they all had no tail at all."

"Zat is the zing, madam, it's a mutation, a mutation of zer spine you see, some of zem have no tails at all but some have a leettle short, stumpy tail."

The woman seemed to be an expert on the subject and Sarah and Elisabeth thought it wise not to argue.

"Oh," they said, nodding together.

"Hallo, my name is Doctor Eva Schmidt," said the lady, stretching out her hand which was at least as wrinkled as her face. It was shaken by Geli, Elisabeth and Sarah in turn, "and I'm a veterinary you see, I specialise in small animals, hamsters, dogs and cats."

"Ah," the Beckers nodded in unison, everything was becoming much clearer.

Dr Schmidt was very friendly and interesting and she was very easy to talk with, so the group chatted quite happily as they sat.

Rumours and tittle tattle were rife amongst the ladies. Amongst the Jewish refugees, who had already spent the past six to ten months escaping across Europe from the tide of fascism, rumours were circulating that they were to be taken to the Isle of Man and once there they were to be put onto German ships and sent home into Hitler's clutches.

Other groups of ladies who sympathised with Hitler's regime were gossiping about the possibility of being returned to Germany, but this time to a hero's welcome. When they got back to the Fatherland they thought they would be able to go straight to the German intelligence service and give them lots of vital information about Britain which would help Germany win the war.

There didn't seem to be any other Americans to talk with so the Beckers, and Dr Schmidt, who seemed to be above tittle tattle, didn't have anyone to share any gossip with.

It was now almost seven thirty at night and the police who had collected the Beckers had been right when they said they wouldn't know where their next meal would come from! They hadn't eaten a single thing since they had left south London and now they were all starving. The only people who had eaten anything all day were babies who seemed to have had an endless supply of bottles of milk. Sarah's stomach was rumbling and grumbling loudly along with many others.

"Come and get it! Come and get your bread and butter!" yelled an old lady who was banging furiously on a rusty old tin tray, well at least she looked like an old lady to Sarah Becker!

"Bread and butter!" squirmed Sarah, "Ugh! I've not had my dinner yet! Why would I want just bread and butter? What sort of a meal is that? Do they think we're pigs?" Sarah thought the old lady who was shouting out was deaf too, but she found out that she wasn't.

"Pigs?" she yelled furiously, "pigs? I'll give you pigs! You'll get what you're given, like it or lump it you little minx!" cursed the woman angrily, waving her blunt butter knife menacingly at her. If her hand had slipped the knife would have been launched across the room in their direction and even though it wasn't sharp it could have taken somebody's eye out!

"Shh! Come on, Sarah, let's go and get some food," whispered Geli putting a comforting arm around her granddaughter's shoulder, "it's better than nothing you know and it'll fill you up, you know what that policeman said when we left London."

"Mmm, alright," grumbled Sarah reluctantly.

20

"Ja, it ees better zan nozzing, Sarah," agreed Dr Schmidt philosophically, "I zink you'll feel better when you've had somezing to eat."

"Yes, but bread and butter, Dr Schmidt!" protested Sarah holding up her hands dramatically.

"It is better than nothing, Sarah," snapped Elisabeth, who was worrying nonstop about Jacob, they'd been split up by the police at Euston station and she hadn't seen him since, "listen to Grossmutti, you must remember what those police said this morning, you've got to have food when you can, you don't know when you'll eat next! There's a war on, remember!"

"There isn't a war on in America!" snapped back Sarah furiously, who noticing the tears in her mum's eyes as she spoke quickly changed her tone, "Sorry, Mom. You're worried about Jacob, aren't you?" Sarah whispered in her mum's ear.

Tears started flooding into Elisabeth's eyes, "He's so young, Sarah."

"He is young," said Geli putting a comforting arm around her daughter in law, "but Jacob, he's a tough boy, Elisabeth, he'll be alright, I'm sure we'll see him and Carl so very soon."

But Elisabeth Becker wasn't so sure. It was true her son was big for his age and he was always acting the tough guy but he was still only twelve years old. Still a child.

Sarah and Geli tugged Elisabeth to her feet and they met up with the patiently waiting Dr Schmidt.

They had just set off for their tea and suddenly they stumbled across a little girl who was curled up tight on the floor at the feet of an older lady. The girl was sobbing and she seemed completely heartbroken. The lady was trying to pick her up but she just curled herself up tighter and tighter like a hibernating door mouse! She had made herself far too heavy for the woman to move.

"Lassen Sie uns essen! Lassen Sie uns essen!" screamed the older women at the poor child, who had her hands clamped over her ears to block out the sounds all around her.

21

"Hey! Maybe she ain't hungry!" yelled Sarah, the American in her flooding out. She rushed over to defend the girl, who was now being kicked and prodded by the lady, who was smoking all the while, "Hey lady! Stop! Stop kicking her! Stop hitting her! Stop it at once!"

By now Elisabeth was by her daughter's side and they managed to pull the older woman away and stopped her lashing out at the young girl.

When they got a closer look at her they discovered that the girl was only about eight years old and looked very frightened.

The woman lunged out once again.

"Hey! Stop kicking the girl!" threatened Elisabeth angrily, "She's got rights you know!"

"Rights!" the woman yelled back furiously, in poor English, "Rights! What rights do zeez children have?"

"Everyone's got rights!" argued Sarah.

"Well you can look after her," snapped the woman angrily, "I'm not even related to her, I'm just doing a favour for her family who are still in Germany and I don't need zee upset! Heavens! Isn't it enough being sent to prison because you are German wizout having to look after someone else's child?"

The Becker party looked at her with blank expressions. There was no way that the woman was going to get any sympathy from any of them!

"Oh! Very well! She's all yours then!" the woman stormed off to get her helping of tea and bread and butter, "You look after her, I wash my hands of her!"

When Sarah, Elisabeth and Gelli looked more closely at the skinny dark haired girl they noticed she was very pretty. She was wearing a scarlet pinafore dress and her long hair was tied in pigtails. But she was still curled tight as a ball and sobbing uncontrollably.

"Sind Sie gut?" asked Elisabeth.

"Don't speak to me in German," sobbed the girl, "it's all their fault!"

"Who's fault, dear?" Asked Elisabeth gently.

"The Germans! I hate the Germans!" She looked up, her red eyes full of heavy salty tears.

"It's not the fault of all the Germans, my love," replied Geli softly, stroking the girl's hair.

"Yes it is!" snapped the little girl bitterly, "I hate being German, it's their fault! All of this, this war, the killing, being sent to that terrible little island! All of it! I don't want to go! What will happen to my friends? I won't be there to go to school with them," the girl started sobbing again, mumbling, "It's all the fault of the rotten Germans!"

"Oh, my little love," cooed Geli, continuing to gently stroke the child's hair, "all this, the war, the killing, this is not down to Germans, we are Germans and we're not killing. Are we?"

"Then whose fault is it?" cried the girl, sadly, a questioning look on her face.

"It's the fault of the Nazis..."

"What? Like them," nodded the girl in the direction of some women who had on black shirts with makeshift arm bands with the Nazi symbol, the swastika, drawn on them in red lipstick.

"Yes," Geli shook her head, "like them."

"Mom," whispered Sarah, "what does it mean, that sign, the sign of those Nazis."

"Ah, Sarah, well a sign doesn't mean anything, and it can't hurt anyone, it's what people think it stands for."

"And what does it stand for now, Mom?"

"The Nazis, my dear."

"And Hitler? That man with the funny thing on his face?"

"You mean his moustache?"

"Yeah!" continued Sarah, "the funny little moustache, Jacob says it's just like a little caterpillar that's crawled onto his face!"

Suddenly the little girl started chuckling, she was still sobbing a little but she was chuckling nevertheless.

Sarah looked at the girl, and continued, "a fluffy, hairy caterpillar..."

The girl started laughing properly now, she was no longer crying.

"... a big fat, hairy, horrible caterpillar!" Sarah went on and on making fun of Hitler's moustache.

"Or a hairy, furry smelly slug!" laughed the girl, joining in enthusiastically.

"I bet his face is all slimy, too?" chuckled Elisabeth, adding her thoughts.

Everyone, including Geli and Dr Schmidt were now roaring with laughter and causing everyone to stare at them.

The Nazi women were staring especially hard at them, giving them the 'evil eye', they didn't like anyone having fun or laughing. To them, like Mrs Freidrich, laughter and fun were 'verboten'!

"Bread and butter, come and get your bread and butter!" screeched the old lady furiously, "It's nearly all gone!"

"Come on," Elisabeth helped the girl to her feet, "we should get something to eat and drink before it's all gone, come on, you can come with us."

Chapter 7

U.S. EMBASSY, LONDON

Carl Becker had spent hours and hours at the Ministry of War trying to find out the fate of his family. All day he'd been passed from pillar to post by one official after another. He'd called in favours and had finally discovered that his family were on their way to an Alien Internment Camp called the Rushen Camp, which was on the very south western tip of the Isle of Man in two small adjoining villages called Port St Mary and Port Erin.

Carl's argument that his family were American citizens

didn't seem to carry much weight at all at the Ministry of War and eventually he'd made his way over to the impressive American Embassy building at 1 Grosvenor Square in Westminster, right at the heart of the city of London.

Then, just after three pm a kindly young clerk called Jane Daniels had taken pity on Carl and ushered him into her office to see what she could do to help him.

"So, Professor Becker," she said "I understand your family have been taken into custody today," Daniels had a strong American accent which comforted Becker after his hours of arguing with some stubborn Brits. For some reason he instantly felt Daniels could be an ally.

"They've been arrested!" Carl was unable to hide his anger, he was sick of all the words, 'custody', 'alien', 'internment', his family had been arrested.

"On what charge, Sir?" replied Daniels calmly, she was well used to dealing with people who were upset.

"On no charge!"

"Please! Please don't shout at me, Professor," protested Daniels calmly, "I'm just trying to understand what's going on."

"Sorry," said Carl, suddenly ashamed of his behaviour towards a lady. Carl Becker didn't normally shout at anyone let alone ladies.

"It's OK," continued Jane Daniels, "but I don't quite understand why they've been arrested."

"They've been arrested because my family has German origins, my mother, Geli, she was actually born in Germany, but I wasn't, I was born here in Britain, and so was my wife Elisabeth and so were our children."

"OK, OK, let me just take some notes first of all, Professor," Jane Daniels opened her desk drawer and took out a writing pad and a pencil and prepared to take notes, "OK, so your full name is?"

"Professor Carl Jacob Becker."

"Carl Jacob Becker," repeated Daniels carefully making notes, "and you say you're an American citizen now, Sir?"

"Yes, here's my passport," Becker passed his American papers over and Daniels methodically took some notes from it.

"And your wife is called?"

"Elisabeth Sarah Becker."

"And she's an American citizen too?" Asked Daniels.

"Yes."

"You have two children? What are their names?"

"Jacob Becker, he's my son and he's twelve, though he looks a lot older, he looks at least sixteen, heaven knows what they've done with him, probably sent him to an adult camp, I should think!" This was the worst fear of Carl Becker.

"OK, and your daughter?"

"She's called Sarah Becker and she's ten."

"And you mentioned your mother?" Daniels was a very thorough clerk and didn't want to miss anything.

"Yes, her name is Geli Becker."

"I take it she's not an American?"

"No, she's a British citizen."

"But she's German born, am I right?"

"Yes, mam. She used to live in Liverpool but moved to London when we went to America, so she could be part of the German community. She has no other family apart from us."

"And you say that they were taken into custody yesterday morning?"

"Yes, whilst I was at the Ministry of War meeting with some people, I'm working on..."

"Sir, please!" She held her hands up to stop Becker speaking, "I don't think I need to know what you're working on, Professor," Daniels smiled, "I assume it's top secret?"

"Yes, mam, sorry, you're right, it is. Err, my wife left this."

Carl Becker took Elisabeth's note from his inside jacket pocket and passed it over. Jane Daniels read it carefully and took more notes, stopping briefly to sharpen her pencil!

"OK," she said, finally folding up the letter and handing it back, "I'll have to make a few calls, so if you wouldn't mind waiting outside my office for a few moments, Sir?"

The wait out in the corridor seemed endless for Carl Becker, the minutes ticked slowly by but eventually after almost forty five minutes Jane Daniels' door opened and she poked her head and beautifully coiffured red hair around the door frame and smiled.

"Could you come in please, Professor?"

Once inside the office Daniels beckoned for Professor Becker to take a seat once more.

"OK, Professor, I have some information for you. Your wife, mother and children have been arrested under a new law called the Internment of Aliens Act..."

"But we're not aliens, were Americans!" yelled Becker angrily.

Jane Daniels took a deep breath, "Professor Becker, please!"

"Sorry."

Daniels sighed and spoke softly, "Professor Becker, you must understand, the United Kingdom is at war with Germany..."

"But we're not Germans!" Argued Becker.

"I know, I know, but the country is in turmoil, Poland has been invaded, France has been invaded, people are worried that Britain could be next!"

Carl Becker let out a deep breath and sat back in his chair feeling utterly deflated, "OK, so what next?"

"I've just spoken to Dame Joanna Cruikshank, she's the commandant at the Rushen Camp, where your family are being taken, and she's promised that she'll look out for your family."

"I want to go and be with them!" declared Carl Becker leaping to his feet.

"I've also," continued Jane Daniels calmly interrupting the academic, "spoken with Professor Stanley Geller at MIT, and he's promised to..."

Suddenly the black phone on Jane Daniels desk roared into life, ringing loudly.

"Ah," said the clerk, "that will probably be him now..." She picked up the receiver, "Hello, Jane Daniels...ah, Professor Geller,...good...he's here now, I've explained everything...I know...I know, he wants to go to the Isle of Man to be with them...understandable yes. Sure, OK, would you?" Jane Daniels put her hand over the receiver and spoke to Becker, "Professor Geller would like a quick word with you."

"OK," Carl Becker reached out for the phone and slowly sat down, "Hello."

"Carl," said a familiar voice on the other end of the line, it was just after lunch time back in Massachusetts.

"Stanley, thank goodness!" It was nice to hear a familiar voice amid the turmoil of the day.

"So, how are you bearing up, Carl?"

"Not too good to be honest, so level with me, Stanley," said Carl cutting to the chase, "what can we do about all this?"

"Well," sighed Geller dramatically, he was prone to being dramatic, "to be brutally honest, Carl, not a heck of a lot, but for what it's worth, I think that your folks will be safe and sound on the Isle of, where did you say?"

"The Isle of Man."

"Sure, the Isle of Man. It is after all in the middle of the Irish Sea so it sure won't be a target for the Luftwaffe."

"But they'd be safer back home in America."

"That's true, but you're needed there, Carl, you gotta understand, this is vital work you're doing, not just vital for the British but vital for us too, you don't think old Adolf is gonna stop with the Brits do ya?"

"I don't know," Carl was feeling utterly deflated and couldn't think straight. His head was swimming.

"Well I don't, Carl! He won't stop. Like it or not, sooner or later Uncle Sam won't be able to stay sitting on his fence this side of the pond, soon we're gonna get drawn into this war whether we like it or not!"

"I suppose," mumbled Becker quietly.

"There ain't no suppose about it!" Geller said firmly, "And we need you there at Bawdsey working in that team! It's crucial, Carl! Vital work! It could save millions of American and British lives and stop us all ending up speaking German!"

"But I want to be with them, Stanley."

"I understand that, Carl, you're a father and husband, and a darn good one at that! But you're needed at Bawdsey. Listen, Miss Daniels has told me she's spoken with the Commandant on the Isle of..., where was it again?"

"The Isle of Man!" Carl rolled his eyes.

"Sure! And, anyway, she says they'll be just fine over there. Look it'll be like a nice little holiday for them, they'll enjoy it, what's not to enjoy? A nice break by the beach! Trust me, Carl, have I ever lied to you?"

"Well..."

"No 'well' about it, Carl," continued Geller, "you're needed at Bawdsey, that's all there is to it! So let Miss Daniels sort out your train ticket and you need to get yourself out of London quick smart, my friend." Professor Stanley Geller was his usual table thumping self, "there's no time to waste, Carl, but you gotta keep in touch with Miss Daniels, you promise me?"

"Promise," sighed Carl.

"Good! When she can she'll sort a visit to the Isle of..., where did you say again?"

"Man," sighed Carl Becker, "the Isle of Man, Stanley!"

"Right! She'll sort out a visit to the Isle of Man."

"OK, bye," sighed Carl Becker slowly passing the phone back to Jane Daniels.

Jane Daniels did sort out a train ticket and an Embassy car for Carl Becker and as late afternoon turned into early evening he made his way across London to Liverpool Street Railway Station and the early evening train to Ipswich, where he would change trains and travel on to Felixstowe, which was close to Bawdsey.

At the port of Felixstowe Professor Becker would be met by representatives of the research institute and they would have to wait for the small boat to arrive to take them over to the top secret secluded research establishment on the Suffolk coast at Bawdsey Manor.

Chapter 8

AN ARRIVAL UNFIT FOR A LADY

Elisabeth, Geli, young Sarah, Dr Schmidt and their new friend, who they discovered was called Laila Levy had travelled overnight on the steam ship the SS Snaefell from Liverpool to Douglas along with over fifteen hundred other women and children.

Whilst many slept for some, like Elisabeth, sleep was impossible. Elisabeth hadn't slept a wink and had been up on deck watching the late spring sun rise shortly before five a.m.

It had been an exhausting twenty four hours for the thirty four year old mum of two. Every time she felt herself dozing off something, some noise, some voice, cough, whisper or snore had woken her. She'd spent half the night making sure her ten year old daughter, her new found friend and her sixty five year old mother in law were alright. The other half she'd spent wondering where on earth her precious twelve year old son and beloved husband were. No, tonight, sleep was not an option for Elisabeth Becker.

The noises were the worst thing for Elisabeth. She was used to sleeping in a peaceful pretty white bedroom in her large whitewashed clap board wooden house in New England, not on a huge, rusty old steamboat lumbering across the rough Irish Sea with hundreds of other women and children.

Apart from Geli and Dr Schmidt snoring like two earthquakes rumbling away all night, there was the droning of the engines deep below them and the creaking of the ship carrying it's human cargo. There were babies crying, children having nightmares and waking up screaming and shouting and, always, the relentless noise of the ship chugging along through the sea.

Eventually, Elisabeth had finally given up on the idea that she could get any rest at all.

"Mommy! Mommy!" Elisabeth could hear her daughter calling for her as she stood on deck watching the tiny speck of land to the west grow ever larger in the distance as the ship neared its destination.

"Mommy! Mommy!" The call was getting louder.

"I'm here, darling!" called Elisabeth, peering for her daughter.

"Mommy! Mommy!" She sounded upset.

"Sarah, I'm here, honey!" Elisabeth set off to find her daughter through the meagre straggle of bleary eyed individuals who couldn't sleep either.

"Oh! Mommy! There you are!" Sarah said, bumping into her and hugging her tight.

"Yes, I'm here, I'm sorry I left you, but you, Grossmutti, Dr Schmidt and Laila were sleeping so peacefully that I thought you might sleep for hours."

"We can't, not now, they're waking people up. And I was worried because when I asked one lady where you were she said that you'd jumped into the sea."

"She said what?" Elisabeth was angry, "Point her out to me when we go down below and I'll give her what for!"

"Oh, it doesn't matter now, Mom," said Sarah calmly, "I already told her to shut up and not to be so stupid!"

As Sarah led the way down below deck she smiled to herself at the thought of her ten year old daughter putting a fully grown woman firmly in her place!

After everyone had queued for ages for the bathrooms and toilets to clean themselves as best they could, the internees had faced a breakfast of yet more tea and bread and butter.

Just as everyone had finished eating, the ship started pulling slowly into the harbour at Douglas, the capital of the Isle of Man.

It seemed to take hours to get into the port, the ship was shunted back and forth by small fat tug boats until eventually it was in just the right position to unload its unenthusiastic cargo of women and children who desperately wanted to be somewhere, anywhere else.

As the ship moored, the night was slowly departing and in its place was dawning a warm, sunny morning. Everyone was encouraged to line up in an orderly manner to disembark and Sarah grabbed her mother's hand.

"Laila," she ordered forcefully, "take Grossmutti's hand, quick!"

Elisabeth, Sarah and Laila had to carry what possessions they had brought with them and very soon it felt like their arms were going to drop off because it was a very long walk along the jetty to the place where a small stream train was belching out black smoke as it waited for its passengers.

Even though she felt tired and worried, Geli didn't complain because she felt luckier than many people who had been completely separated from their families. Although she hated everything that was happening, she was with her family. However, the train journey and the sea crossing had exhausted her and the last thing she wanted was a long walk in the increasingly warm May sunshine.

Chapter 9

FELIXSTOWE

Professor Carl Becker had arrived at Felixstowe late in the evening and a heavy sea mist had meant he'd had to delay the final part of his journey along the coast to Bawdsey Manor, which had to be made by small boat.

He'd been met from the train by the most amiable and enthusiastic person he had ever met in his whole life, a smart young lady who introduced herself to him as Charlotte Smith.

"Professor Becker? Professor Becker?" called the pretty young blonde woman, who was dressed in smart civilian clothing, as the scientist stepped off the crowded train from Ipswich.

Thick, acrid smoke was belching from the train and floating along the busy platform. At first Carl Becker couldn't see who had called his name, the platform was so crowded. People were shouting and calling out and it was altogether a very confused situation.

"Yes? Hello!" Carl called to no one in particular. "Hello!"

"Oo hoo!" the voice was getting louder, trying to get the academic's attention, "Professor Becker! Oo hoo! Professor Becker!"

"Excuse me? I'm here!" responded Carl, craning his neck to see who was calling his name.

"Here I am, Sir!"

A pretty, smiling face appeared right in front of Carl as if by magic, "Hello there, Professor Becker? How do you do?" The woman was very jolly indeed.

"So very nice to meet you, Sir," the young lady shook his hand with an extraordinary amount of strength which he hadn't anticipated. She was constantly babbling away, "How do you do?" she asked once more, "My name is Charlotte Smith and I've been sent to meet and accompany you over to Bawdsey Manor but I think, to be quite frank, we may have a small problem tonight. It happens like this sometimes here, nothing at all to worry about."

"Oh, right," a sleepy Becker rubbed his eyes, the events of the day had finally caught up with him after he changed trains at Ipswich and he'd dropped off to sleep on the short ride over to Felixstowe on the final train journey of the day.

"Did you nod off on the train, Sir?" Questioned Smith.

"Err, yes, yes I must have done," Carl stifled a yawn.

"Easily done, Sir, I do it all the time, it's not too much of a problem when your destination is the end of the line like this but if it isn't...," Charlotte Smith starting shaking her head dramatically and tutting, "then you can have quite a problem indeed."

"Yes, I suppose so," agreed Becker, looking all around at the vibrant scene that he was caught up in.

The train had been crowded with soldiers who'd been laughing and joking and telling tall stories. It hadn't been too bad in first class where he had his seat but in second and third class it looked chaotic.

Now the platform was full. Troops of all shapes and sizes manoeuvred their way around civilians and found their way to waiting army trucks amid the black smoke from the train which hung low over the platform and the mist that was rolling in from the North Sea.

"It's busy here," noted Becker as he was jostled by some troops carrying rifles and back packs.

"Sorry, mate!" said one of them.

"It's OK," replied the Professor.

"Yes, it's a very busy place, Professor," Smith pulled Carl by the arm and took his suitcase. "This way to our car."

"No, no don't, I'll carry that," protested Carl.

"Don't worry, Sir, I'm much stronger than I look!" laughed Smith brushing off his protest, "Look," she pointed, "that's our car just through there."

At the car, a large black Austin 12 with all its lights blacked out except for tiny thin slits on the headlamps, Smith placed Professor Becker's case in the boot at the rear of the vehicle before rushing around to open the rear door for her guest.

"I'll sit up front if that's alright with you," said Carl, he was a bad traveller and easily got car sick, the only solution he'd ever found that made it better was to sit in the front seat.

"Certainly," replied Smith shutting the rear door and opening the front passenger one.

"I get car sick you see," explained the Professor.

"Ah, I see," Smith thought for a moment or two, "doesn't chewing gum help at all? I'm so sorry but I'm afraid I haven't any, actually haven't seen any for ages and ages, rations and all that. Haven't seen quite a lot of things actually, still we've all got to make sacrifices if we're to whip Jerry's backside!"

"I've got gum," Becker took a small packet out of his jacket pocket, "but it doesn't help me, doesn't seem to stop the travel sickness at all."

"Oh, I can't remember the last time I saw gum," mused Charlotte, her eyes peering down at the gum longingly.

"Here," said Carl passing the small packet over, "have it."

"Oh, no, I couldn't. I'm so sorry I wasn't..., I'm sorry, I don't want you to think that I was..."

"I don't! Please, take it, I don't want it, don't particularly like it. My wife got it back home, she likes it you see."

"Well, if you're sure."

"Sure I'm sure, please, have it."

It was getting quite dark as the new Austin 12 made its way across the Suffolk coastal town of Felixstowe, dodging armoured vehicles, troop trucks and supply vans as the sea mist was growing worse and worse.

"Pea souper tonight!" noted Smith peering through the windscreen.

They made their way all around the large commercial docks and soon the damage caused by German bombing became apparent to Carl.

"From what I can see, it looks like Felixstowe has suffered a lot," Becker stared at the depressing view.

"It's had more than its fair share, Sir," replied Smith. "Not as bad as some but more than its fair share."

"Is it bombed here every night then?"

"No, no not every night, about once or twice a week we get a raid, but thanks to our chaps up there," Charlotte pointed to the sky, referring to the Royal Air Force, "it could be a lot worse. And tonight the weather will stop any chance of bombing. I'm afraid...," Charlotte pulled up and parked the car in front of a large hotel, "it also means we can't go over to Bawdsey tonight sir, so I'm afraid we will have to stay here at the Marlborough."

The Marlborough was a large and comfortably furnished hotel and when Carl Becker drew back his curtains at five thirty the next morning he discovered it was situated right on the sea front.

For a long while, as the sea mist disappeared in the strong early morning sunshine, Carl thought about his family. Where were they? What were they doing? His beloved wife Elisabeth, his children Jacob and Sarah and his mother Geli. Were they safe? Were they actually already on the Isle of Man at the Rushen Camp or whatever it was called? Or were they on a boat at sea running the risk of being torpedoed by a rogue German submarine? Carl knew that there were submarines patrolling in the Irish Sea and they had destroyed ships that had been unlucky enough to find themselves in their sights. Carl shivered at the thought.

Knock, knock!

The sound of someone knocking on his door dragged Carl out of his daydreams

"Sir!" whispered a woman's voice, "Sir! It's Charlotte Smith here. Sir, you need to wake up, get dressed and have a quick breakfast. We need to set off for Bawdsey, we're due to leave within the hour."

"It's OK," replied Carl quietly so as to not disturb any of the other guests, "I'm awake, Charlotte, I'll be down in five minutes."

"Very good, Sir."

Chapter 10

JACOB'S DOCKSIDE PRISON

Morning was fast approaching when Jacob Becker started to come round. At first he couldn't think where he was, and for a few wonderful moments he was back in his own bedroom in the family's large four bedroom house, complete with his smooth haired Jack Russell dog Snowy laid out next to his bed snoring lazily. Snowy liked to sleep late and Jacob always had to wake him for breakfast. He loved to share Jacob's eggs and toast with him.

Soon Jacob would be getting up to go to school, where he would see all his friends, share a joke, play some ball and maybe learn something from their teacher, Mrs Jackson, about what was happening in the war that was raging in distant Europe.

"Wanna drink, mate?" slurred a strange voice and Jacob was brought firmly back to reality with a bump, "Wanna drink?" the voice repeated.

"Err, what?" Jacob's head was spinning but his eyes seemed glued tight shut. Try as he might he couldn't prise them open, "Dad? Dad?" he mumbled slowly, "Is that you, Dad?"

"Wanna drink?" The someone was forcing a cup to his mouth now, "Come on, mate, have a sip! You gotta be parched. Gotta be."

Without thinking Jacob started drinking, drinking and drinking. He didn't realise how thirsty he was. His throat felt like sandpaper he was so dry. He couldn't remember the last time he'd had a drink, but there again he couldn't remember much at all, and he couldn't remember where on earth he was.

"Hold on a minute, mate," said the voice taking the empty cup away, soon it was replaced with a full one. "Alright, you can drink again now."

Jacob gratefully drained the second cup too and then a third until he wasn't thirsty any more.

Strong hands propped him upright. Slowly Jacob started to open his eyes. It was starting to come back to him. His worst fears were about to be confirmed and he desperately wanted to go back to sleep and return in his dreams to his peaceful bedroom in Concord, Massachusetts.

Slowly he peered through half closed eyes.

Whoa! Jacob thought. What a sight!

A spotty young man with a feeble attempt at a beard and moustache was sat next to him on the side of a narrow bed. He had another cup of water ready to offer Jacob.

They were sat in a small, oblong shaped room. It was just long enough for two narrow beds and wide enough for someone to walk between the beds. If you stood up and stretched your arms out you could almost touch the side walls.

The dim light of morning was seeping feebly through a small window high on the wall next to the head of Jacob's bed. Looking up, Jacob noticed that the window had bars on it. It was a jail.

Oh no! He thought. Everything was coming back to him now.

"Where am I?" moaned Jacob, rubbing his head.

"Are you American?" asked the boy, grinning, as if an American was something from outer space or someone from the movies!

"Yeah...Where are we?" Jacob didn't think he had picked up much of an accent back home because all his friends referred to him as the English kid!

"Jail, mate."

"Jail! What jail? Why? Where?"

"Dockside jail, Liverpool docks, dunno why you're here though, me, I escaped and went on a bit of a bender. I nicked a tug boat, almost got it out of the river and into the sea I did too, but they caught me and threw me in here! In the slammer!"

"Slammer?"

"Yeah, slammer! Gonna throw the book at me they said when I get over on to the island! Ooh, I'm sooo terrified!" mocked the lad sarcastically. Despite everything he had a big cheeky grin on his face.

Jacob couldn't help but like the look of the lad who didn't seem at all bothered that he was in jail and seemed to be taking it all in his stride.

As Jacob got a closer look at the young man he didn't look as old as Jacob had first thought, maybe only a few years older than him.

"Terry!" he declared, sticking a dirty hand in Jacob's direction and reading Jacob's thoughts, "I'm Terry Lowe."

"Jacob," replied Jacob, cautiously shaking Terry's outstretched hand, "Jacob Becker."

"Well Jacob, Jacob Becker, what is a young American lad doing here, most likely on his way to the prisons on the Isle of Man like me? You don't sound very German to me!"

"Neither do you! Are you German?" asked Jacob, taking the cup of water from Terry and sipping gratefully. Terry didn't sound at all German.

"Me dad's German," declared Terry, "well he was born in Germany, been over here for years and years, from well before even Moses was a lad!"

"Moses?" asked Jacob, "Moses...what?"

"Yeah, have you never heard that one, Jake?"

"No," Jacob shook his head which ached terribly. He winced.

"They must have hit you over the head," noticed Terry.

"They...?"

"The coppers, the coppers must have bashed you over the head when they arrested you."

Jacob felt his head properly, there was a big bump there, "Yeah, they must," agreed Jacob, rubbing his head gingerly. It really hurt.

"But," continued Terry, oblivious to Jacob's discomfort, "our real name isn't Lowe at all, it's Loewe, that's German."

"Oh?"

"Yeah, Dad changed it when he first moved to England twenty years ago. Germans still weren't that popular over here then. It was after the Great War you see and Germans definitely were not the flavour of the month after the sinking of the Lusitania, so he told everyone we were Dutch. Not many folk in Skipton could tell the difference so we were fine. He did well actually, really well, we're cobblers you see, well we were, until that idiot came to power!"

"Idiot?" Jacob didn't understand.

"Hitler!" Terry spat out the name.

"Oh, right. Yeah he is an idiot! I hate him," Jacob really meant it.

"A right lunatic! Anyway a week ago there was a knock on the shop door one morning before we opened up. Right early it was. An ungodly hour my Mum said. In fact she refused to get out of bed so they had to drag her out kicking and screaming!"

"They dragged your Mom out of bed?" Jacob was thinking that maybe it hadn't been so bad for his family. The police that came for them made them tea and toast whilst they packed. They even let his Mum call home to America and tell the Green's next door that they might have to look after Snowy for a while longer. The police were quite kind to the Becker family and even said they didn't like taking them away. It went fairly well until they split them up at Euston Station and put them on different trains. Jacob was still angry at that. His mum, Elisabeth, had been so upset.

"Yeah!" laughed Terry, "Carted us all away they did. Anyway they split us up in Bradford, me, mum and dad, I haven't seen them since...err...the day before yesterday I think. I haven't a clue where they are. At least they're safe from that mad man, Hitler," Terry spat on the ground in disgust as he said the name again, "I suppose that's something."

"Then what happened?" asked Jacob curiously.

"Well, Jake, they were going to put me on a ship, that big ship over there," Terry stood up on Jacob's bed and pointed out of the window, "can you see it? What's its name? I can't see it too well, I must need specs."

Jacob got to his feet, still feeling drowsy and climbed up to the window, "err...Rushen something I guess."

"The Rushen Castle? That's it, The Rushen Castle!" continued Terry, "Funny name for a ship, what's Russia got to do with anything?"

"It's not..." Jacob tried to explain they were different spellings but Terry continued his tale.

"Anyway they were gonna take me straight to the Isle of Man they were but I wasn't having any of it, not bloomin' likely!"

"You weren't?" Jacob replied, sitting back down on his bunk. Terry joined him.

"No way, Jake! I boarded with everyone else, right sly I was, and then I jumped ship, hid out a while, found a bar, had too much gut rot..."

"Gut rot?"

"Booze, too much to drink!"

"Oh, OK," Jacob rubbed his sore head again, at least Terry's story was taking his mind off his own problems.

"Then I decided to find a ship to take me to America!"

"You were going to go to America?" gasped Jacob, "kinda like a stowaway?"

"Yeah, course! People do, you know!"

"Mmm, I suppose."

"Like what's his name!" Asked Terry.

"Who?"

"Robin somebody?" asked Terry.

"Robin somebody?"

"Aye, Robin...Robinson Crusoe!"

"Oh," sighed Jacob as Terry continued, "Robinson Crusoe... but I don't think he was going to America..."

"No? Anyway when I couldn't find anyone to take me I thought why not try and sail one across myself. I mean, how hard could it be, it's only what, a few miles?"

"A few miles?" Jacob couldn't believe what he was hearing.

"Yeah! Well they do call it the pond don't they, Jakey boy?" Terry grinned. "Everyone knows that!"

"But I think that's just a nickname, Terry," said Jacob quietly.

"Is it?" Terry's grin was fast disappearing, "are you sure?"

"Yes, very sure. Terry how far do you actually think it is to America?" Asked Jacob.

"A few miles, I suppose," shrugged Terry, "twenty at the most."

"Twenty? It's thousands and thousands of miles, Terry!"

"Is it?" Terry had a shocked look on his face, "are you sure, Jake?"

"Yeah! Very sure! It's thousands of miles! But they stopped your boat did they?" asked Jacob, desperate to find out what happened next. Talking to Terry made him forget his own problems just for a little while.

"Yeah they did..." sighed Terry, "...and maybe if what you're saying is right, Jake, that was probably for the best!"

"Mmm...maybe."

"Well," continued Terry, "I suppose thinking back I could have chosen a quieter moment, but there again I had me beer goggles on didn't I!" Terry laughed, and Jacob had to chuckle, "Big thick, blurry beer goggles!"

It was the first time Jacob had laughed out loud for ages.

"Oh well." Sighed Terry, "Hey! But what about you?"

"Me?"

"Yeah! Do you know, you're a bit of a legend around here," he said changing the subject to Jacob, "and you've only been in here a few hours too!"

"What?" scowled Jacob, not having a clue what Terry was talking about. He couldn't remember very much at all about what had gone on last night.

"Breaking out of a prison van, and escaping!"

"Well..."

"Folk are saying they had to bring in policemen from as far away as Manchester and Leeds to catch the fast boy, you, cos no one here was quick enough!" chuckled Terry, "Now I know why you're so fast."

"You do?"

"Yeah, everyone knows Yankees are fast runners."

Jacob suddenly felt really proud of himself.

"How did they catch you in the end?" asked Terry, "Did you slip or something? You must have slipped, must have,

there's no way they could have caught you without you slipping! Not Yankee Boy."

"Yeah, I slipped!" grumbled Jacob, rubbing his sore head.

"Then they whacked you over the head?"

"Must have." Jacob closed his eyes and slowly laid back on the small, uncomfortable bed

Chapter 11

BAWDSEY MANOR

It was at least a mile and a half from the hotel to the small jetty, where a battered looking fishing boat was moored patiently awaiting the arrival of Professor Carl Becker and Charlotte Smith. Smith insisted on driving the academic who really wasn't used to all the royal treatment that he was currently receiving.

It was still very early in the morning and the sea mist had yet to lift completely on the large sea port, giving the morning a slightly eerie, ghostly feel. The sound of gulls squawking and screaming as they dive-bombed the beach, fighting and squabbling amongst themselves for their breakfast, sounded strangely human as Becker and Smith got out of the car. Becker shivered without thinking.

"Are you cold, Sir?" asked Smith as she retrieved his case from the boot of the car.

"Err, what?" Becker was thinking about his family, it was all he could think about, all of the time, not whether he was cold or not.

"You shivered, Sir."

"Did I? Oh, yes, so I did. Cold? No, no, I'm not cold, it's just those sounds, the sound of the birds screaming."

"Oh that, they do sound awful don't they?" Smith was jolly even at this ungodly hour, "Look," she nodded, "this is our boat."

"Oh, is it?" Carl Becker didn't have sea legs and a journey on a small boat, no matter how short, didn't fill him with much enthusiasm.

"Not a good sailor either?" smiled Smith curiously.

"No," he shook his head, "I don't like boats very much."

"Don't worry, Sir, it's very calm this morning, like a duck pond, and it's not such a long journey, less than twenty minutes."

Suitcases were lifted on to the boat by a surly fisherman and Professor Becker was helped on by the confident Smith who had athletically leapt across.

"Err...is there a life jacket or something?" asked Carl, sitting down at the back of the boat, anxiously looking around.

"Nay, ya don't be wanting a life jacket!" laughed the fisherman, who had leathery tanned skin the colour of dark oak. Thick, curly silvery hair escaped from under a moth eaten old woolly hat. His skin so contrasted with his hair and eyes that in the gloom of early morning all that could be seen were tufts of hair and the whites of his eyes.

"I don't?"

"Naw, we won't be more than five minutes at sea, lad, then we'll head up the Dreben estuary for the last few minutes, it's not far and we'll never be more than fifty yards or so from the land. If ya fell overboard you could almost walk back to the land."

"Really?" remarked Becker, "walk you say?"

"Oh, you'll be fine, landlubber!"

"Mmm..." murmured

"Cast off will ya?" the skipper called over his shoulder.

"Would you mind, Sir?" asked Smith, "I can never untie his blooming knots. They're far too tight for me."

Carefully and reluctantly, Carl got up and tentatively felt his way back across the small boat. He just hated the way the ground beneath his feet was always moving on boats, as if he was skidding and sliding across a bowl of jelly and custard. He hated the feeling and it made him feel sick even before he'd cast off!

"Hurry up, lad," called the skipper, revving the engines impatiently.

Carl climbed carefully back onto the jetty. "Ah!" He sighed. How good it felt being on dry land again and he hadn't even put out to sea yet! Carl Jacob Becker certainly did not have sea legs!

Carl fiddled around with the rope which was tied to the jetty. Charlotte had been right, the knot was impossible.

"I can't undo it!" called Carl after a couple of minutes of struggling.

"Can't undo it, landlubber?" repeated the skipper with a toothy mocking grin, "Well I never, who'd have thought it?"

However, the mocking made Carl all the more determined to get the rope undone and then he could get on with the last leg of the journey and get off the blasted boat.

He manically fiddled and fumbled and to his great relief after a long couple of minutes the knot finally slackened. "Got it!" he called triumphantly.

"About time, landlubber! Quick, throw the rope back and hop over."

The boat's engines were roaring and the boat was beginning to move away from the dockside.

"Hurry up, Sir!" encouraged Charlotte, her arm outstretched, "Quick! QUICK!"

Carl took a gulp of the fresh, salty seaside air and took off. He seemed to be in mid air for an age.

"Ha ha! Don't look down, landlubber!" chuckled the skipper.

Carl didn't heed his advice. As he jumped he did look down, and there was sea beneath him, actual water! Swishing about violently between the boat and the jetty! Carl suddenly felt light headed but he seemed to automatically stretch out his hand and somehow he miraculously caught Charlotte's. With assured confidence and super strength she pulled him on board the small vessel and he landed in a crumpled heap at her feet feeling altogether embarrassed.

"Are you alright, Sir?" Said Smith looking down at him.

"Ha ha ha! He'll be alright, lass, leave him on the floor, that way he won't be sick!" The skipper was shaking his head and tutting, "I don't know, you landlubbers!"

"Oh, I wouldn't bet on not being sick," muttered Carl who was slowly going very green around the gills. He was beginning to wish he hadn't had kippers for breakfast.

When Carl finally did look up the boat was ploughing slowly north up the coast, headed for the mouth of the Dreben Estuary.

"Look over there!" beckoned the skipper, who was pointing towards the land with his pipe.

"Where?" asked Carl.

"At the cliffs, lad!"

"Oh OK."

"Does tha know there's history in those cliffs?"

"History?"

"Aye fossils, lad, fossils of creatures that lived here millions and millions of years ago."

"Oh yes," Carl remembered now, "I remember, they're Pleistocene."

"Plysto what?" replied the Skipper, expertly lighting up the old pipe with one hand while never taking his other hand off the steering wheel for an instant.

"Pleistocene," repeated Carl.

"Nay nay, lad," the skipper puffed and puffed on his pipe, weighing up the scientist suspiciously, "they're nothing like that, nothing of the sort, they're rock!"

Carl decided it was best not to argue with the burly fisherman who slowly turned the boat to head up the steadily flowing river estuary all the while savouring the aromatic pipe.

Very soon the boat started gradually slowing down.

"There it is, Bawdsey Manor!" pointed Charlotte Smith.

"Aye that's Bawdsey alright," agreed the Skipper.

Carl looked in the direction where Charlotte was pointing and there, slowly rising out of the mist was the ghostly shape of a large impressive castle-like manor house. It had ornate spires with green topped copper roofs and was of a red brick construction.

"It was built in 1886," explained Charlotte, "and then enlarged in 1895 by Sir William Cuthbert Quilter."

"Oh, I don't think I've heard of him," Carl shook his head.

"Ah, that's because Sir William wasn't a landlubber tha knows," added the Skipper helpfully.

"No?" replied Carl.

"Actually," continued Charlotte, "he was a famous art collector and the Member of Parliament for Sudbury too."

"Really?"

The boat made its way slowly towards a private jetty that jutted right out into the river. The Skipper eased off the revs and then turned the engine off completely.

"Got to save fuel!" he grinned, his pipe firmly stuck between his teeth, "There is a war on this 'ere side of t'Atlantic, tha knows."

The Skipper wasn't the first person to make a comment to Carl Becker about America's refusal to join the fight against Hitler and, no doubt, he wouldn't be the last.

The coasting boat was expertly steered into the wooden jetty, which was surrounded by old tyres tied on by rope, and the craft slowly eased up to a gentle stop.

"Rope, landlubber!" ordered the Skipper.

"Sorry?" said Carl.

"Rope! Tie her up! Quick!"

Carl clambered up onto the jetty and while he was still crawling around on his hands and knees, tied the rope on firmly.

"Reef knot, if you please!" called the Skipper.

"But I don't know how to tie a reef knot," protested Becker.

Instead of replying the Skipper just shook his head and tutted making his way towards the rope clutched in Carl Becker's hand

"Professor Becker?" came the sound of a male voice approaching.

Even before he had chance to stand up the man was right on top of him. Standing well over six feet tall, the heavily built man had long white hair, a bushy white moustache and a long white beard. He looked a lot like Santa Claus but was wearing a brown tweed sports jacket and not a bright red coat.

"Yes?" replied Carl Becker, scrambling to his feet.

"Jim Wilson!" boomed the man in a voice that could certainly have been that of Father Christmas.

"Oh!" sighed Becker finally, "Professor Wilson?"

"No formalities around these parts, Carl, just call me Jim, everyone does. Hold on," he peered into the boat, "do you need a hand with that lot, Lottie?"

"No, I've got it thanks, Jim," replied Charlotte climbing out onto the jetty.

"Well, Jim, it's nice to meet you," Carl shook Wilson's outstretched hand.

Carl thought he was going to pull his arm out of its socket as Jim shook his hand vigorously!

"Welcome! Welcome! Welcome to Bawdsey! I do hope you'll be very comfortable here." Wilson looked over his shoulder back into the boat, "Are you on your own?"

"Sorry?"

"Your family not with you? We've been expecting them, I thought they were coming over from the States too?

There's plenty of room for them here, Carl! They'll be safe and sound. No need to worry."

"They did come Jim...it's a long story."

"Ah, a mystery? I like mysteries! Do tell."

"They were...well, Jim,..." Carl sighed, "...they were arrested," even the words were hard for him to say.

"Arrested?" Wilson scowled, "Sorry about that, old boy."

"Well, not actually arrested, they call it interned."

"Interned?"

"As in 'internment of aliens' interned!" explained Carl.

"Ah," paused Wilson, things were becoming clearer, "I see...I had read that the politicians back in old Londinium were becoming a little over sensitive about things, didn't think it had come to this though, thought they were out to find and bang up any fascist sympathisers that's all?"

"So did I, so did a lot of people, but apparently not anymore," continued Becker, "anyone, man, woman and child that has any links whatsoever with Germany is being rounded up and sent to internment camps."

"My goodness! My goodness me!" Wilson shook his head, "I thought we lived in a free country!"

"Mmm...me too!"

"What is the world coming too, Carl? Do you by any chance know where they've been taken?"

"Oh yes, they're either at or on their way to the Isle of Man."

"The Isle of Man?"

"Yes."

"Well, I suppose that's the place you would send prisoners you didn't want to escape. Didn't they do this sort of thing in the Great War?"

"I don't know, yes, yes, I think they did."

"They had a great big camp over there with a funny sounding name didn't they? Now let me think, what was its name?" Jim Wilson produced an old pipe out of his jacket pocket and stuck it in his mouth. He didn't bother to light it but just sucked on it instead and it seemed to assist his brain searching, "That's it!" he said shortly, "It was called Knockaloe! Funny old name, Knockaloe! Once heard, never forgotten! Anyway, anything I can do I will, maybe you can get a pass to go and see them?"

"The American Embassy is trying to organise something."

"Well, I'm sure if anyone can sort something out it's the Yanks! Oh," he paused, "err...sorry old chap, forgot that you were a Yank too these days, old boy! Terribly sorry!

I'm always putting my foot in it!"

"Oh don't worry about it, Jim, so…" Carl Becker looked up at the impressive manor house, "…you're not slumming it down here are you?"

"No, no!" chuckled Wilson, "It's even more impressive inside my boy. Well, shall we have a short tour before coffee and then get down to work, there really is so much to do to complete the radar network before old Adolf decides to try and invade?"

Wilson started walking slowly up to the manor house, followed by Becker and Smith.

"Do you actually think he's going to try?" Whispered Becker.

Jim Wilson suddenly turned around and grabbed Carl by the arm and quickly walked him out of earshot of Charlotte and the boat skipper, then he started whispering too.

"I don't 'think' old boy, I know. One hundred per cent certain."

"You know?"

"Yes, take it from me, before the end of the summer the Luftwaffe will mount the biggest series of air sorties the world has ever seen on our air bases and cities."

"For what reason?" asked Carl.

"Well dear boy, they will be trying to clear the way to destroy the Royal Navy in the Channel. No RAF means no air cover for the ships, and no air cover means that the Navy is, in effect, a sitting duck! And then the path will be clear for them to invade."

"My goodness!" Becker was shocked, "so it's that serious?"

"Indeed! That serious! This information comes from our highest source in Berlin. Let me tell you, invasion is not a matter of if, Carl, it's when."

"I didn't realise time was so tight."

"That's why you've been asked to come over and help now, Carl, we don't have much time left, we need the radar early warning system not only working but networked in a failsafe way so if Jerry does disable part of it, the rest can cover the breakage until it's repaired. This is vital work, Carl, absolutely vital!"

Chapter 12

THE TRAIN

Sarah enjoyed the train journey much more than Elisabeth or Geli, mainly because she had found a new and interesting playmate in the form of Laila.

As soon as they had eaten yet more tea and bread and butter, Laila had started to talk and she chatted almost nonstop from that point onwards!

Although Sarah and Laila spoke German fluently, neither of them liked doing so and neither of them liked listening to the groups of German women chattering and moaning either.

Apart from being worried about the whereabouts of her brother and dad, Sarah was really quite enjoying the whole adventure in which they had found themselves.

And although Laila was desperately worried about her parents she was really enjoying having a playmate around all the time.

Though the journey seemed endless, it had definitely improved for both girls since Laila had come along and now it felt like they were going on holiday because, being an island, the sea and lovely white beaches seemed to be almost everywhere.

The scenery on the Isle of Man was so different to the countryside in America and much different to the endless streets and houses of London. It was so green. There was field after field after field, divided by miles and miles of hedgerows, with only small villages or hamlets to break up the lush greenness.

It seemed like they were a million miles away from any threat of war.

"Don't go too far!" called Elisabeth after her daughter, who had asked if she could go and explore the train.

"No, we won't!"

"And come back before we get to where we're going!" shouted Elisabeth, "Where are we going to, Mutti?" she asked Geli, as she sighed heavily.

"The end of the world!" replied Geli yawning, she was so tired and ready for a comfortable seat.

"Well," the girls heard Dr Schmidt explaining, over the sound of Geli and Elisabeth yawning, "zat's not entirely true..."

Sarah and Laila were desperate to get out of the cramped carriage and so they had decided to ask Elisabeth if they could explore the train.

Curiously, they wandered almost the entire length of the old carriages, having a look in the funny cramped toilets, opening the windows and smelling the aroma of seaweed that seemed to just hang in the air. They nosed about and looked in all the compartments, but every single one was the same, women, women, women! There wasn't a single man on board. Just a few very young boys and they were boring.

And everywhere women sat quietly staring out of the window whilst others tried to keep their children amused, some grumbled loudly and others cried.

Being young and excitable Sarah and Laila busied themselves exploring the rickety old train and didn't give much thought to the passangers who were upset. Although as they walked along Sarah stopped and stared for a moment at a lady in one of the carriages as she passed who was crying as she showed photographs to her neighbour and she thought of how her own family had been separated and for a brief moment sadness engulfed her. But when Laila shouted for her to follow she dashed off further up the train in pursuit of her new found friend.

Most of the children were quite young or even babies so both of the children were glad that they had each other for company.

"Hey you two! You'll have to go back to your compartment now, young Misses," said a jolly looking guard with a smile, he was quite round and wobbly, with a tiny cap perched on his head at an odd angle which looked as if it was about to drop off at any minute!

"Why?" asked Sarah innocently.

"Because we'll be getting to Port Erin soon."

"What's Port Erin?" asked Laila.

"That's where you're going to be staying, Miss. Actually, that's where I live. Are you American?" he asked Sarah.

"Yes, Sir," replied Sarah politely, "and I know the Oath of Allegiance too."

"Oh, you do, do you?" Mr Simpkins the guard had never met a real life American before, but he loved American movies, he could listen to this girl talk all day as he loved the accent.

"Sure."

"Go on then!" He urged.

"OK," Sarah put her hand on her heart and started to recite the American Oath of Allegiance solemnly, "I hereby declare, on oath, that I absolutely and entirely renounce and abjure all allegiance and fidelity to any foreign prince, potentate, state, or sovereignty of whom or which I have heretofore been a subject or citizen; that I will support and defend the Constitution and laws of the United States of America against all enemies, foreign and domestic; that I will bear true faith and allegiance to the same; that I will bear arms on behalf of the United States when required by the law; that I will perform non-combatant service in the Armed Forces of the United States when required by the law; that I will perform work of national importance under civilian direction when required by the law; and that I take this obligation freely without any mental reservation or purpose of evasion," Sarah took a deep breath, she always forgot to breath when she recited the oath, and had gone red in the face, "so help me God."

When Sarah had finally finished, the crowd that had gathered around her started clapping and cheering. Sarah dramatically bowed to her audience.

"Vy are you here, child?" enquired a woman in a strong German accent, "You're American!"

"I don't know, Mam," replied Sarah.

Beep, Beep, whistled the train as it started slowing down.

"Come on now," said Mr Simpkins, "on your way you two, we're arriving," said the guard, ushering Sarah and Laila gently forward, "back to your carriage. There'll be plenty of time for performances later."

Chapter 13

BOARDING THE SHIP

"Come on now you scallywags! Let's be having you!" bellowed a big fat policeman as he pulled his keys, which were on the most enormous key ring so huge it actually weighed one side of the man down, from the lock on Terry and Jacob's cell door and pushed it wide open.

"Where are we going?" asked Terry, who remained stubbornly sat on his bunk with his arms folded across his chest.

"Less of your cheek, lad!" replied the Guard.

"I'm American," added Jacob confidently, "I shouldn't be here."

"And I'm from Timbuktu! And I should be here either," replied the guard, "I should still be in bed at this hour!"

"Where are you taking us?" asked Terry.

"I'm not taking you anywhere lad, and shut up asking questions, just follow me unless you want to feel my truncheon on the back of your head!"

Reluctantly, Terry and Jacob followed the policeman.

"I wonder why he hasn't bothered to cuff us," whispered Terry.

"Do you think I have good cause to?" replied the guard without turning around, he must have had bat ears! "I don't think even you two reprobates would be that stupid!"

"What do you mean?" said Terry innocently.

"Where would you run to, fat lad?"

Outside the prison they could clearly make out the impressively large bulk of The Rushen Castle on the dock side.

"Cor...big innit?" muttered Terry to Jacob.

Black smoke was belching from the ship's one and only chimney or stacker and blowing out towards the sea.

"That's not big, Terry," replied Jacob, "the one we came across the pond on had three stackers!"

"Three?"

"Yep."

"Three?"

"Yes, Terry, three."

The Rushen Castle was flying the flag of the Isle of Man Steam Packet Company and was a trusty workhorse that had been commandeered into taking interned aliens over to the island. After this last trip over to the island she was due to sail down to the south coast of England to be on standby as a troop and supplies ship in case she was needed.

It looked like the ship was full, men crowded the railings up on the deck as Jacob and Terry were escorted to the dockside.

At the base of a ramp a man was sat at a desk with a clipboard, with a list of names that seemed to go on and on forever.

"Name!" he barked at Terry.

"Terry Lowe."

"Terry who?"

"Lowe."

"Lowe, Lowe, Lowe," the man repeated as he searched through the list for Terry's details.

Terry tried to be helpful and started spelling out his name for the man, "L...O..."

"Cheeky blighter! I know how you spell Lowe, lad!" snapped the man who continued searching, "Ah, there you are! Age?"

"Sixteen."

"In your dreams! Up you go, lad." The man turned his attention to Jacob, "Name?"

"Jacob Becker," replied Jacob.

"Funny accent that!" said the man, looking Jacob over suspiciously, "Where are you from, Jacob Becker?"

"Concord, Massachusetts."

"Massachusetts? Massachusetts, America?" The man's eyes narrowed.

"Yeah."

"An American?"

"Yes."

"So how come you're here, lad?"

"You tell me!"

"He's a cheeky one this, Sid!" said the fat policeman butting in.

"So I see, Eric," replied the clerk looking through the list for Jacob's name, "can't fi nd anyone by the name of Becker, Jacob on my list."

"That's because I shouldn't be here, that's why!" argued Jacob.

"How old are you, Becker, Jacob?" asked the clerk.

"Twelve."

"Twelve!" yelled the clerk nearly falling off his seat, "did you hear that, Eric, the lad says he's twelve."

"Never in a million years, Sid!" replied the policeman, "If he's twelve then I'm a monkey's uncle!"

"Well his name isn't on my list, Eric, what do you think?" asked the clerk.

"Must be a mistake, they wouldn't have sent him to us if he wasn't a German, would they?" replied Eric the policeman.

"I'm not supposed to allow anyone to board the ship unless they're on this list," said Sid.

"Well I think we should send him over, Sid, then if they've made a mistake I'm sure they'll send him back, that way we won't get into trouble."

"Well, I don't know," mumbled Sid the clerk, "you know I like to do things by the book, Eric."

"I know, I know, Sid, but what if he is supposed to be on the list and there's been a clerical mistake, what if he's a German spy or something and he tells Jerry some vital information? What if the Luftwaffe bomb Liverpool tonight because of information he's sent back to old Adolf? What if your house gets bombed and your whole family is killed?" Eric was very persuasive.

"Well...if you put it like that, Eric," replied Sid, who'd had his mind made up for him, "on you go, lad."

"But you can't!" argued Jacob as Eric pushed him up the boarding ramp, "I'm American and I'm only twelve!"

"Away with you lad!" said Eric, "You're not American and you're definitely not twelve! If you're twelve," he laughed, "my friend Sid here's twenty one!"

"Twenty one times three more like!" chuckled Sid, "I've heard it all now," he mumbled, "American and twelve years old, ha! Not in a million years."

Chapter 14

THE WOMEN'S CAMP. SARAH, MUM AND GRAN ARRIVE

Port Erin and Port St Mary were small villages right at the southernmost tip of the Isle of Man and if anything seemed even further away from the threat of war than the rest of the island, which seemed a million miles away from the threat of invasion by Hitler's vast armies!

"Sarah, Laila!" called Elisabeth Becker, "Come and help me, Grossmutti and Dr Schmidt with our cases!"

Blonde haired Sarah grabbed two suitcases, like her brother Jacob she looked a lot older than her ten years, she was a tall, strong and sporty girl and easily managed to lug the heavy cases off the train. Laila was much smaller but she helped Dr Schmidt with her cases the best she could.

"These cases are very heavy, Dr Schmidt?" she sighed as she tried to heave them up.

"If they are too heavy, Laila, leave them," said Elisabeth, aware that Laila was very small for her age, "here, let me feel them."

Elisabeth felt the weight of the cases and could barely lift them herself.

"My goodness, Dr Schmidt, what have you got in these cases, rocks?" she half joked.

"Not rocks, Elisabeth, books," replied Dr Schmidt.

"Ah," sighed Elisabeth.

"Books about what, Dr Schmidt?" Asked Laila.

"About veterinary science of course," replied the Dr matter of factly.

Elisabeth helped Geli off the train. The small platform was incredibly crowded. There were hundreds and hundreds, maybe thousands of lost looking worried women stood around with huge suitcases, bags, sacks, one or two even had large tea crates full of their possessions which they could in no way move!

One lady had a large bird cage full of bright yellow canaries. She wasn't the only person with animals. Quite a few people had cats in baskets and there was the odd dog too.

The weather was unexpected for the Isle of Man and most of the women hadn't thought the conditions would be so clement. As the day had moved towards lunchtime the sun had continued to shine as it climbed higher and higher in the sky. It was getting very hot and this was made far worse as most of the women were wearing far too many clothes because they couldn't fit any more into their cases!

A few yards away along the platform a young pregnant lady got so hot she started to faint and then she fell straight over.

Dr Schmidt was the first person to rush over to the lady.

"What's the matter with that fat lady, Mom?" asked Sarah.

"First of all she's not fat, Sarah, she expecting a baby," corrected Elisabeth, who was starting to feel hot and bothered herself because she had two coats on, a thin summer coat and her heavy winter coat, "and secondly I expect the heat and the journey have all been too much for her, in her condition."

"Make way! Make way!" shouted Dr Schmidt to the crowd that had turned and was staring, "Make way, I'm a Doctor."

"Doctor?" whispered Laila to Geli, "I thought she was a vet?"

"Well, people are animals too you know, Laila," replied Geli, who was watching as Dr Schmidt brought the lady round and made sure that she was alright.

A crowd of British ladies and some guards rushed to help Dr Schmidt and before too long an ambulance had pulled up and she was lifted carefully into the back.

"Be careful wiz her!" ordered Dr Schmidt, "She's fragile!"

There was much confusion as the ambulance slowly made its way away from the station.

"Listen up, please! Listen up, please!" called a woman with a loud voice trying to bring the crowd to order.

Of course, she could barely be heard above the din so she moved back to her car, opened the door, leaned in and pressed the horn, over and over.

Hoot! Hoot! Hoot! Hoot! Hoot! Hoot!

Everybody stopped chattering and stared at the woman.

"Thank you!" shouted the woman, standing up on a soapbox, "I am Dame Joanna Cruikshank, Commandant of the Rushen Camp. Now I know you have all had a long journey but if you will all follow me...you will assemble outside St Catherine's Church Hall...you will line up and in single file you will enter the hall...there you will find out where you are to be billeted."

"What does billeted mean, Mom?" whispered Sarah.

"Where we will stay, honey," whispered Elisabeth back.

For the benefit of some of the German ladies who couldn't speak English very well, another lady then translated what Dame Joanna had said, before everyone set off in a very orderly manner following the two ladies.

Chapter 15

RADAR - THE SECRET WEAPON

The top class surroundings at Bawdsey Manor were truly luxurious and sumptuous, just like a five star hotel. As he settled into his large room, which had an attached bathroom, Professor Carl Becker couldn't help but feel guilty at being such a terrible father or at least so he thought.

Here he was living the life of luxury at a plush manor house and there were his family, prisoners in a prisoner of war camp somewhere on the Isle of Man, probably living in huts with dirt floors and eating gruel and dried bread. They were probably chained or manacled in some way too. Oh, how Carl Becker felt like he'd let his family down.

Knock knock! Someone was at his door. When Carl opened it there was the familiar jolly figure of Charlotte Smith.

"Settling in a little, Sir?" she asked, delivering the rest of his belongings and bringing an armful of fresh towels and some nice toiletries, "When you have a moment, Professor Wilson would like you to come down and have coffee and croissants with him on the veranda."

"I didn't think you could get much coffee this side of the Atlantic, and croissants?" noted Carl.

"Oh, chef makes the croissants himself, he's French you see, and you needn't worry, Sir, there's no rationing here, not at Bawdsey."

Five minutes later Carl Becker joined his new employer on the large, impressive veranda on the sunny east side of the manor house. The sea mist had lifted and the morning was now warm and sunny. The garden was full of beautiful flowers which were buzzing with insect life. Birds were chattering in the trees and close by, cows could be heard in the neighbouring fields. It was an idyllic scene of a perfect English country house.

Carl had decided to change into his smartly pressed cream linen suit and pale blue cotton shirt, he'd decided that it was too warm to wear a tie though he had one in his pocket if Professor Wilson insisted.

As he viewed the scene before him, a beautiful house with a fantastic chocolate box garden, tables and chairs set out on the large veranda for morning coffee, he still couldn't believe there was a war raging just a few miles away on the other side of the English Channel and he felt terribly guilty about everything.

"Ah, there you are, Carl! I do hope the room is to your liking?"

"Liking? It's fantastic, Jim, absolutely fantastic! Just like a five star hotel, not that I've stayed in any five star hotels! I just can't believe there's a war on across the water and here we are living like this."

"We're living like this," snapped Professor Wilson, his manner suddenly changing, he now had a stern look on his face, Carl must have hit a nerve, "because we work extremely hard at this establishment, Professor, and the work we are doing here might just well make the difference to us winning or losing this stupid war!"

There was a difficult silence for a couple of minutes until Carl cautiously broke it.

"I'm sorry, Jim, sorry for what I said. It was insensitive of me. I'm new here and I don't know the score."

"Ah..." sighed Professor Wilson, calming down, "I'm sorry for being so touchy..." He lit his pipe and took a long suck on it, "... if the truth be known I think we all feel so terribly guilty."

"Guilty?"

"Yes guilty. Guilty for living in such a beautiful place, Carl. Guilty that while we are here living like this, our boys are over there, he pointed out to sea, "fighting and dying for our country. Guilty that thousands of people in our cities and sea ports are living in constant fear of being bombed by the Luftwaffe night after night. Guilty, terribly guilty."

"I suppose what we need to do is to just do our very best, with our work I mean," said Carl.

"Yes, yes, absolutely we must!"

"If we do our very best we can give our boys and everyone else in this beautiful country a real advantage over the enemy."

"The radar advantage?"

"Yes, the radar advantage!" said Becker.

After coffee and croissants, the mood picked up as Professor Wilson took Carl Becker to see the high tech research facility at the manor. "As you know," said Jim, "the clever thing about our radar system is that it is networked. We now have radar receivers all along the south and the east coast of the country. And it forms a shield, very much like an ear to the skies, if you like"

"Yes, and I understand that it is working very well."

"It is working very well indeed, Carl, and it will give us a major advantage over the enemy, it will buy our boys time to be ready, but we have one problem."

"What is it?"

"You know that Jerry already knows about our radar network?"

"Mmm...I guessed they would, I guess there are spies everywhere," said Carl.

"Yes there are. But they don't know everything about radar, or fully understand its potential, but they do know enough."

"Enough to what?"

"To target it. Bomb it."

"You think they're gonna attack the network?"

"Oh yes, without a shadow of a doubt they are, if it were us in their position we certainly would."

"Yeah, I suppose. So what are we going to do about this, if radar is targeted and goes down then we'll lose the advantage of seeing the Luftwaffe coming."

"Precisely."

"So," asked Carl again, "what are we going to do about this?"

"Not we, Carl, you, what are you going to do about this?" Professor Wilson smiled.

"Me?"

"Carl, that's the reason why we've brought you all the way across the Atlantic, you're going to make the system failsafe. One part of the chain breaks another part takes its place! Over compensates so to speak. You, Professor Becker, are a communications expert not a radar expert, it's your forte, Carl. We need our network to be fully operational all the time, we need it to be constantly communicating even if half of it goes off line. You're here, Carl, to fix our problem and make sure we keep our advantage over the enemy."

Chapter 16

SAILING ON THE RUSHEN CASTLE - TO THE ISLAND IN THE MIDDLE OF NOWHERE

There were hundreds and hundreds of men on the Rushen Castle. It wasn't a massive ship but it was full to bursting.

Many of the men were actually German, many of them were Jewish refugees who had spent months and months travelling to escape from persecution at the hands of the Nazis. Many of these poor people were in a very bad physical and emotional condition, and many of them didn't speak very much English.

Almost as soon as Jacob boarded the ship, the gangplank was raised and the Manx sailors pulled in the ropes that moored the ship to the dock. Yet more filthy black smoke belched out of the stacker and the Rushen Castle's engines rumbled and roared to life making the whole ship shudder and shake.

Terry was waiting for Jacob as he boarded the ship.

"Are you OK, Jake?"

"Nope, not really," tears were in Jacob's eyes, and this emotion belied his age.

"Was that true what you were saying to Laurel and Hardy down there?"

"What? About being an American?"

"No, even I can tell you're an American," laughed Terry, "no, what you said about being twelve?"

Jacob snuffled into a handkerchief.

"Well, Jake?"

"Yeah, it's true," sobbed Jacob quietly.

"Wow!" said Terry with a look of admiration in his eyes.

"What?" Jacob was confused.

"You really are a legend, Jacob Becker, not only are you the fastest man, sorry boy, in the north west of England, but you're only twelve! Good grief! And I thought I looked old for my age."

"Why? How old are you?" asked Jacob.

"I'll only tell you if you promise not tell a single soul."

"I promise."

"Cross your heart."

"Cross my heart," repeated Jacob sighing.

"And hope to die."

"Well I aint gonna say that, Terry! Not even for this," replied Jacob firmly.

"Oh right, fair enough," said Terry, "but you do promise don't you?"

"Yeah, I promise," Jacob was getting a bit fed up with Terry's questioning.

"I'm sixteen and a half."

"Sixteen!"

"And a half!" Terry was so proud of the half that Jacob couldn't help himself having a little laugh!

"Hey! What are you laughing at?" asked Terry.

"You! 'and a half'!" mocked Jacob, laughing.

"Shut your face, schooly!" joked Terry.

"Shut yours, shoe bum!" replied Jacob.

"Yankee bum!" replied Terry.

They both enjoyed a good laugh at each other. Jacob could tell he was going to be good friends with Terry Lowe.

Over the ship's tannoy the captain announced that a basic breakfast of tea, bread, butter and jam was to be served just as soon as the ship broke away from its mooring.

Realising that they were feeling really hungry Jacob and Terry ran down below decks to stand and queue and line up along with everyone else.

As they approached the servers, Jacob and Terry noticed that a man slightly ahead of them in the queue was having difficulty understanding what was going on and what he was being told to do.

"Oy! Just two slices each!" bellowed the serving man behind the counter, "Weren't you listening? You can't take three! Just two! There's a blooming war on you know!"

The man in the queue was very skinny and sickly looking who, although not that old, looked like he'd been going through really hard times recently. He looked very dirty and exhausted and had just picked up three slices of bread and butter instead of two.

"I no understand," protested the man shrugging his shoulder pathetically, "I no understand," he kept repeating this over and over.

"I already told you! You can't take three slices, mate! Watch my lips, THERE...IS...A...WAR...ON! Only two, TWO!" To try and make himself understood he was shouting louder and louder and this was only making the man seem even more confused, "WATCH MY LIPS! TWO!"

"I no understand!" repeated the man.

"Are you stupid or something?" the man glared at the pathetic looking, hungry individual opposite.

"Excuse me, excuse me!" By now Jacob had had enough! "Let me pass! Excuse me!" He hated bullies and when it was obvious that no one else was going to stand up and do something he decided he wasn't going to let the situation continue. He had to help. He quickly pushed his way to the front of the queue, nobody bothered to stop him because everyone was scared of the man handing out the food and they certainly did not want to risk making him any angrier, but not Jacob.

"Oy you! No queue jumping!" yelled the server, waggling a butter knife at Jacob.

"Hey, dumb butt!" roared Jacob, "Can't you see he doesn't understand you?"

"That's because he's a stupid Nazi kraut!" spat the man who was going very red in the face.

"He's not a stupid Nazi at all! Wait!" replied Jacob, who then turned to the man and explained in German that there was a limit of only two pieces of bread and butter each, but that he could have jam on them if he wanted. He asked the man a few questions about where he had come from and his name and what he did for a living.

After a short while he turned back to the man behind the counter who was rolling his eyes in exasperation.

"This man's name is Helmut, and he's not a Nazi at all, he's a Jew and he's come all the way across Europe on foot trying to escape from the Nazis and to look for safety in England."

"I didn't know that," argued the server quietly, looking down, suddenly feeling ashamed of the way he had behaved.

"He also says," continued Jacob calmly, "that he had to escape because the Nazi soldiers came to his house one morning and took all his family away. They rounded them up at gun point, even his ninety year old grandmother and baby nephew and made them get into big cattle trucks. He doesn't know where they are or even if they're alive!"

"How was I to know that?" argued the server pathetically, still unable to look anyone in the eye.

"And actually he's a waiter, too, in a cafe back home and where he serves, people can take as much as they want, there is no limit. He was hungry and he wanted three slices, that's all."

The server was going even redder in the face as he realised how stupid he was being made to look and how unkind he had been, feeling truly ashamed of his behaviour.

"Look, I'm sorry, I really am, I didn't know all of that about his family, can you do me a favour?"

"Err..." replied Jacob.

"How do I apologise in German?" asked the man.

"Oh...err, say 'entschuldigungen'," replied Jacob, who was feeling relieved.

"What?"

"Entschuldigungen. Listen, just repeat after me...Ent"

"Ent," repeated the server.

"Schul"

"Schul"

"Dig."

"Dig.

"Ungen."

"Ungen."

"Entschuldigungen," repeated Jacob putting the parts of the word together.

"Entschooldeegungin!" said the man.

"Near enough," said Jacob.

"Danke, danke!" said the Jew nodding his head towards the server, who then took Jacob's hand and said quietly in very poor English, "Zank you, my angel."

As Jacob walked away and back to Terry, the man behind the counter called over to him.

"Hey, Yankee, do you want to ask him if he wants a job? I need a hand right now if he'll help!"

Jacob grinned at Terry, "Sure!"

Chapter 17

ST CATHERINE'S CHURCH HALL, BEING SORTED

"Listen please, listen!" The lady paused as the din died down, "Thank you" bellowed the same lady who had honked the car horn at the station.

She had made it perfectly clear who was in charge and no one was in any doubt that she was that person. And for good measure she always had her interpreter repeat what she said in German so that no one had the excuse that they didn't understand what she'd said.

The mass of women and children were stood in a long line outside the church hall of the pretty St Catherine's Church, and once again Dame Joanna was stood on her soapbox, which at least meant nearly everyone could see her.

"Ladies and Children! You WILL queue in an orderly fashion, and you WILL enter the church hall in your small groups, you WILL then receive the instructions as to where you are to be billeted. AND...Listen up now! I don't expect any trouble! I hope that is CLEARLY understood!"

Everyone chattered excitedly about where they were to stay. The small villages seemed to have more than their fair share of signs and notices for this hotel and that guest house. It was definitely a place used to catering for lots of visitors.

But Port St Mary and Port Erin didn't look very much like a prison camp to Sarah and Laila and no one could see any fences or walls to keep people in. It just looked like everyone was on holiday and waiting to find out which guest house or hotel they were going to stay in.

"I will shout out your names in alphabetical order and you will then come forward and start to form an orderly queue!" called Dame Joanna, "The faster this is done, the sooner you can all have a rest and something to eat after your long journey."

Suddenly the prospect of proper food made the crowds of people co-operate enthusiastically because everyone was desperately hungry.

"I hope it's not more bread and butter," whispered Sarah to Laila.

"Me too!"

Because Becker begins with a B, Elisabeth, Geli and Sarah were almost at the front of the line. Although Laila should have stood elsewhere, Elisabeth was going to say that she had adopted her and now her name was Becker-Levy.

"Not much longer, Mutti," whispered Elisabeth to Geli, who was looking truly exhausted, "then you can have a sit down and something to eat and drink."

"Here," said Dr Schmidt, who was telling everyone that she had to stay with Geli because of a serious medical condition and no one, not even Dame Joanna, ventured to argue with Dr Schmidt, "have some sherbet! Sherbet always refreshes just like a drink! I often prescribe it, it's miraculous!"

"I thought she was a vet?" whispered Laila to Sarah.

"I think she's making sure that everyone believes she's a person doctor so we all stay together."

"Oh."

In their small groups the families slowly, and in the required orderly fashion, filed into the small church hall.

As they walked in there was a thoughtful lady with hot cups of tea and biscuits ready to refresh the weary travellers.

"Tea and biscuits, ladies?" asked the lady.

"Oh thank you," said Elisabeth, getting a cup for her mother in law and Dr Schmidt, "is it alright if my mother in law sits down over there, Mam? Dr Schmidt here is helping to care for her, while I sort this all out."

Even Elisabeth had picked up an American twang in her years in the States.

"Yes, of course," said a woman sat behind a desk with lots of files and papers, "you are all one family I take it?" She peered over the top of her horn rimmed spectacles at the group.

"Yes and no, Mam. We're the Beckers from Concord."

"Concord?" The clerk was a member of the local Christian Science Church, which is based in America, so she knew straight away where Concord was, "Concord, Massachusetts? America?"

"Yes, Mam," replied Elisabeth politely, exaggerating her American accent, if speaking like an American got her family any perks or even on the first ship back home then Elisabeth would speak as American as President Abraham Lincoln!

"Dame Joanna," called the lady clerk, to the Commandant, who was busy making arrangements with another family.

"Yes, Mrs Hobson?" said Dame Joanna coming over.

Dame Joanna Cruikshank was the founder of the RAF Nursing Service in 1918 and served as its first Matron-in-Chief before being appointed the commandant of the Rushen Camp for women and children at Port St Mary and Port Erin on the Isle of Man so she was well used to taking charge of matters.

"Dame Joanna, sorry to bother you but this lady and her family here are American citizens," said Mrs Hobson.

"Really? An American?" said Dame Joanna, trying to fully remember her conversation with the American Embassy, "Can I see your passports, please?"

Elisabeth being an American citizen did have American passports for herself and her daughter and she handed them over.

"Oh, I see, yes I remember now, the Beckers, and this other lady?"

"This is my mother in law, Geli Becker, she's an English citizen."

Dame Joanna looked at Geli Becker's British passport and then turned her attention back to Elisabeth.

"But you are a German family I take it, Mrs Becker?"

"My mother in law here was born in Germany, yes, but we are an American family. I was born in England. And as far as I remember the United States of America is still an ally of the United Kingdom."

"Ah, I remember now," said the Commandant as everything became clearer, "I have spoken with a Miss Daniels at the American Embassy about you, your husband has been to see her."

"You spoke to my husband?" The thought of any sort of contact with her husband filled Elisabeth with renewed hope.

"No no, I said I spoke with Miss Daniels at the Embassy, I didn't speak directly with your husband, Mrs Becker."

"Oh."

"But it appears that your husband has the highest possible security clearance and is working on a very, very important project."

"Does that mean we will be able to leave and go home?" asked Sarah hopefully.

"Well, I'm afraid not young lady, as I explained to Miss Daniels, I have my orders and whether I like them or not I do have to obey them, the Government of this United Kingdom has decided that all people with German origin, whether they be British citizens, American citizens or people working on special projects, must be detained because of the potential threat they may pose to national security."

"But if my husband..." argued Elizabeth.

"Mrs Becker, because of your husband you are to receive extra consideration and I understand he will, in due course, be coming to visit."

"When?" pleaded Elisabeth, hopefully.

"I don't know."

"And what about my son?"

"Your son?"

"Yes, my son Jacob," explained Elisabeth, tears filling her eyes, "because he looks older than he is, they separated us at Euston Station, I haven't seen him since and I don't know where he is, I'm very worried!"

"I'm sure you are," replied Dame Joanna, "rest assured I will follow this up for you and find out where your son, err, Jacob?"

"Yes, Jacob."

"Where Jacob is. Please don't worry, I'm sure he will be perfectly fine. Now please proceed to obtain details of your billeting."

"But my husband is a scientist working for the Department of War!" reasoned Elisabeth Becker attempting one last throw of the dice.

"And I'm sure that no one involved in that work would thank you for shouting about your husband's role!" replied Dame Joanna quietly, "I am sorry, Mrs Becker, but at this present time, this is the law of this land, please proceed to your billet," she nodded in the direction of Geli, "it certainly looks like your mother in law could do with a rest."

"I'll be in to see you about this," replied Elisabeth angrily.

"I look forward to it."

Chapter 18

THE RUSHEN CASTLE
ARRIVES IN DOUGLAS

It was early evening by the time the Rushen Castle slowly pulled into the port of Douglas, the capital of the Isle of Man which lies on the eastern side of the island. The sea had been calm all day and the crossing had been smooth.

As soon as they left Liverpool the Captain's voice came over the loud speakers and asked for everyone to be watchful for attack by the enemy. Almost every pair of eyes, apart from those men who clearly supported the Nazi regime, had been up on deck for almost all the journey, keeping a close look out for any unwanted attention from German U boat submarines.

Although the Irish Sea was known as U boat alley in both world wars, it was widely acknowledged that most of the prowling submarines would probably be on the look out for convoys of ships that were sailing into the port of Liverpool from America and Canada. These convoys were bringing vital supplies to the British Isles, and they ranged from food to machinery, from weapons to key personnel.

Because they were targeted so fiercely by the German naval forces or Kriegsmarine, trans-Atlantic convoys tended to be extremely heavily protected. They would have many different shapes and sizes of allied warships protecting them and quite often British submarines prowled around hunting for any U boats. Earlier in the year on the 12th of February 1940 in the Firth of Clyde, which was the northern mouth of the Irish Sea,

U Boat Number 33, commanded by Hans-Wilhelm von Dresky, was successfully sunk as it tried to attack a trans-Atlantic supply convoy by depth charge bombs fired from a British minesweeper, HMS Gleaner.

But today there had been no sightings of any U boats, only the heavy presence of the Royal Navy as it made sure the passage into the docks of the north west of England were kept safe and secure.

"Looks funny, doesn't it?" said Terry as he and Jacob stood on deck watching the ship come slowly into port.

"What does?"

"The island."

"Why?"

"Well, it looks funny, a tiny little island stuck right in the middle of the Irish Sea."

"I'd never thought about it before, Terry," shrugged Jacob as they neared the Port of Douglas.

Douglas was a much smaller port than Liverpool, with its shipyards and massive commercial and military docks, and very much smaller than New York where the Beckers had sailed from to come to Britain.

There also looked to be much fewer soldiers, sailors and policemen milling about waiting for them than on the mainland and the ones they could see looked quite old.

"Actually it is a very interesting place, the Isle of Man," a man standing next to them at the ship's railings nodded towards the shore.

"Excuse me?" said Jacob turning round.

"In geological terms."

"Oh," said Terry.

"Yes, in geological terms the Isle of Man is very interesting indeed," continued the man, "it's in a crossroads you see, between the European and the North American plate."

"Plate?" repeated Terry, who was confused, but Jacob knew what he was talking about.

"He's talking about the earth's crust, Terry," clarified Jacob.

"Ja, exactly!" grinned the man, "Well done! Ja, I'm talking about tectonic plates. I must apologise, I always do this, my name is Professor Muller, Dirk Muller, and I'm a geologist."

"Mmm...a rock doctor!" chuckled Jacob.

"Ja, if you like," he stuck his hand out to shake the boys' hands in turn.

"Hi," said Jacob, "I'm Jacob Becker and this is Terry Lowe."

"How do you do?" said Terry, shaking the man's hand.

"Very well considering, Terry," replied Professor Muller.

Chapter 19

MRS SIMPKINS' HOUSE BY THE BEACH

Along with another family, the Beckers, Laila and Dr Schmidt were billeted with Mrs Simpkins, the wife of the railway guard that Sarah had met earlier in the day.

The Simpkins' lodgings was a medium sized six bedroom guest house in village of Port Erin.

Mrs Simpkins was a kindly lady. She was quite podgy but had a pretty smiley face, she always wore make up and red lipstick and wore her long white hair up in a bun on the top of her head.

"Now then, now then," she said, rubbing her hands together with glee as they walked through her garden gate and up the path.

She seemed genuinely pleased to have the visitors stay in her house which was true in more ways than one. She was a grandmother herself and loved to have children around the house, but she was also a seaside landlady and because of the war there weren't that many people visiting the Isle of Man for holidays anymore.

For Mrs Simpkins having German alien prisoners billeted with her meant that at least she was making some money because she got cheques from the government. Her husband didn't earn that much working on the railways and the guest house had always provided very useful income for the family.

"Mrs Simpkins?" asked Elisabeth as she approached.

"Yes dear, that's me!" she grinned as she patted the girls gently on their heads, "Elspeth Simpkins."

"My name is Elisabeth Becker," replied Elisabeth holding out her hand.

"Are you American, dear?"

"Yes, mam."

"Oh how exciting! It's been such a long time since any Americans visited this part of the island, how wonderful! How wonderful!" Mrs Simpkins seemed genuinely overjoyed.

"Mrs Simpkins, this is my mother in law, Geli."

"Hello, Geli, pleased to meet you, dear."

"And my daughter, Sarah."

"Hello, dear."

"Hello," said Sarah.

"This is my adopted daughter, Laila."

"Hello Laila, my, aren't you a pretty girl!"

"Hello, Mrs Simpkins," replied Laila.

"Oh, what very polite girls you are," noted Mrs Simpkins, "it's going to be wonderful having you staying here, I'm sure you're going to liven the whole place up no end!"

"And this is my mother in law's carer, Dr Schmidt."

"Hello, Dr Schmidt, nice to meet you."

"Good morning, madam," replied Dr Schmidt formally.

"Well, I'll show you up to your rooms, I've got another family coming too, oh I think this is them coming now. Hello, hello I'll be with you in just a tick...where was I? Oh yes, I'm sure there's going to be plenty of space for everyone, and I'm sure everyone's going to get on so well! If you take your things upstairs I'll see to these guests, then I'll pop up and show you your rooms and then prepare some lunch for everyone."

And there was indeed plenty of space for everyone. Even when the Schwartzkopfs arrived there was more than enough room for the two families.

The Becker contingent were allocated three rooms in total and one bathroom with a toilet just for themselves right at the top of the tall seaside house. Elisabeth and Geli shared a large twin room overlooking the sea and Sarah and Laila had the smaller room next door which also looked out over the sea. Dr Schmidt had a small, cosy room at the back of the house with the bathroom right next door.

The Schwartzkopfs were made up of a twenty five year old mum, Lily, and a grandmother Eva, with two small four and a half year old twin boys, Ernst and Hans. Lily and Eva shared a room facing the seaside on the floor right below the Beckers and the twins had bunk beds in the room next door. On the same floor at the back of the house was another bathroom and the large room that Mr and Mrs Simpkins slept in. Mrs Simpkins had told everyone that Mr Simpkins didn't like to climb too many stairs so a room on the first floor was perfect for him.

"Mom, mom!" called Sarah as she and Laila ran excitedly into their bedroom, dropped their things down on the floor and ran over to peer out of the window.

"Yes, honey?" replied Elisabeth who was busying herself getting clothes sorted out.

"Can me and Laila go down to the beach and go for a swim in the sea? Can we, Mom? Please, Mom? Can we? Pleeeeease?"

The beach at Port St Mary and Port Erin was stunningly beautiful and as the day was hot and sunny the sea looked so tempting to the girls who had been travelling for a day and a half in cramped trains and overcrowded ships.

"Oh, I don't know about that, Sarah."

"Aw!! Why not?"

"Because we're not here on vacation sweetheart, it's not a time for fun, Daddy and Jacob aren't with us."

"Oh, I know," Sarah was quiet for a while but the activity on the beach was drawing her attention like a magnet, "...but there are people, Mom, ladies that were on the boat are already down on the beach swimming and sunbathing, ooh look, Laila..."

"What?"

"Look!" Sarah was pointing, "...and some of them haven't any swimming costumes on either!"

"OK, OK!" sighed Elisabeth, peering out of her window, "well we'll see after we've had some lunch, honey."

After almost two days of eating just bread and butter all of the visitors, the Beckers and the Schwartzkopfs, were visibly disheartened as Mrs Simpkins walked into the dining room with a huge plate of sliced bread and a large basin of yellow butter.

"Oh no! Not bread and butter," mumbled one of the twins, who were so similar even their mother could barely tell them apart!

Although not wanting to seem ungrateful everyone, without exception, had really long faces as Mrs Simpkins placed the food on the large oil cloth covered dining table. Lily Schwartzkopf glared at her son.

"I'm sorry, is there something the matter?" asked a perplexed Mrs Simpkins.

There was an uncomfortable silence before finally Elisabeth thought she had better speak.

"Ah, I don't really know how to say this."

"Why? What have I done?" Mrs Simpkins looked upset.

"Oh, no! Nothing! You've done nothing wrong, Mrs Simpkins, nothing at all."

"Then what is it, please tell me."

"It's just that...," Elisabeth took a deep breath and nodded at the plates of bread and the butter that were in the middle of the table.

"What, dear?" Mrs Simpkins was confused.

"That," Elisabeth and everyone else nodded at the bread plate.

"I'm sorry but I don't understand, what are you talking about, what about the bread and butter?"

"I'm sorry," apologised Elisabeth once again.

"What about? Spit it out, dear, I can't bear to think that my guests are unhappy about something, it just wouldn't seem at all right!"

"It just that's all we've had to eat for the past two days!" blurted out Laila bravely.

"What? Bread and butter?"

"Yes," everyone replied at the same time.

"Bread and butter?" repeated Mrs Simpkins, who was incredulous, "That's all you've eaten for two days?"

"Yes."

"Oh dear, you poor things, oh...now I see," said Mrs Simpkins slowly, everything was becoming clear, "and now you all think that's all you'll be having here too? Is that it?"

"Yes," replied Elisabeth, a little ashamed, "I suppose."

"Oh you silly, silly things!" chuckled Mrs Simpkins, walking out of the room.

Two minutes later she reappeared with a huge bowl of fresh salad, then she went away and brought in a huge bowl of fresh tomatoes, then cold boiled new potatoes, then hard boiled eggs, then finally she reappeared with a huge deep red coloured dish full of rhubarb crumble.

"By the way, there's homemade custard to go with that too!" she said.

"Oh, Mrs Simpkins," sighed Elisabeth, "I'm so sorry, you must think that we're so ungrateful?"

"Not at all, dear! I think I would probably have reacted exactly the same if all I'd eaten for two days was bread and butter and the first thing that appeared on the table was bread and butter!" She was laughing hard and everyone joined in.

After lunch, Geli and Dr Schmidt went up to their bedrooms for a nap, Mrs Schwartzkopf took the twins for their afternoon sleep too and made the most of the peace and quiet herself. Elisabeth allowed the girls to go and play and swim on the beach while she helped Mrs Simpkins with the clearing up.

Without having to be told twice the girls disappeared off to the beach but reappeared within ten short minutes. They were puffing and panting hard. They must have run all the way.

"We've got a big problem, Mom!" declared Sarah catching her breath.

"What is it, honey?"

"I've just realised that we don't have swimming costumes, Mom?" whined Sarah.

"And we're NOT going to swim with no clothes on!" said Laila firmly, "Some ladies are, but WE ARE NOT!"

"Oh," smiled Elisabeth, "well, I'm sure pleased about that, Laila."

"There's a shop close to the beach and they've got some really lovely costumes in their window. Can we buy some, Mom? Mom? Please! Please, Mom? " pleaded Sarah pathetically, "Laila will pay you back when she sees Mrs Freidrich again."

"I will, Mrs Becker, I will, I promise, Mrs Freidrich has got lots of money from my parents, I'll definitely get some from her for the swimming costume."

"Oh OK, here you go," said Elisabeth, handing over some money, "but make sure you bring me the change."

"Yeah, we will!" said Sarah as they both dashed off, "thanks, Mom!"

"Thank you, Mrs Becker," called Laila over her shoulder.

The shop was quite close to the sea front and sold swimming costumes for men and women as well as for children. They also sold buckets and spades, beach balls and other things for the seaside.

"Hi!" said Sarah as she breezed into the shop.

"Good afternoon, young Miss," replied the man from behind the counter. He was a tubby man and he was wearing a pale green shirt with a bright pink bow tie. He didn't have much hair on his head and the bald bit was extremely shiny. So shiny in fact, that you could almost see your reflection on it. The man was wearing half moon spectacles that seemed to just perch on the end of his nose, "how can I help you young ladies?"

"We'd like to buy two swimming costumes please, Sir?" Sarah was being extra polite because she was really desperate to get the costume quick smart and get into the beautiful sea.

"Ah," said the man staring over at the costumes, "a very wise choice on such a lovely day, Miss, and I must say we don't see too many Americans around these parts."

"No?"

"What colours would you each like?" asked the man, walking past the girls to the clothes rail, "I'm afraid I don't have any with stars and stripes on!" he laughed at his own joke as he rummaged about and then brought out a small selection of knitted woollen costumes that looked about the right size for Sarah and Laila.

There was a brown one which neither of the girls fancied very much because it was too dull.

"That looks like the colour of poo!" mumbled Sarah cheekily in German to her friend who sniggered behind her hand.

Sarah had quickly realised that if she ever wanted to keep things secret she could speak to her friend in German and even though she hated the German language Laila agreed it could be quite a fun thing to do.

"Maybe cow poo!" agreed Laila.

The man looked at the girls blankly, clearly not understanding a single word of what they were saying. He then brought out a black suit, a grey one, a red one and a deep purple one which were more to their taste. The girls looked at each other.

"I would like the purple one please, Sir," said Laila politely, speaking perfect English once again.

"Very good, and you, Miss?"

"The red one for me, please," replied Sarah.

The man carefully wrapped the costumes in two brown paper bags, though the girls wanted to change into them there and then.

"Now then, Ladies," said the man, "do you have any clothing coupons?"

"Clothing coupons?" asked Sarah, looking blankly at her friend, she hadn't even thought she would need anything else apart from money, "No, Sir, I've only got this," she waved a crisp, clean pound note in front of the man, "but my mom says she wants some change."

One pound was far, far too much for the swimming costumes that cost only one shilling and sixpence each with a clothing coupon, but tempted by the sight of it and the knowledge that his shop had not had many sales recently the man thought about breaking the law and making an exception to asking for coupons. Maybe the arrival of hundreds of wealthy German women would make the war a little more bearable for him and his business?

"Oh, there certainly will be change, Ladies, I can assure you of that but if you haven't got any clothing coupons I'm afraid…"

"Oh I don't need much change," said Sarah desperate to get the costume. She handed over the note and the man snatched it from her greedily.

"Well then, I am very happy to sell them to you," the man smirked in a very smarmy way as he started digging into a tin underneath his old cash register. After a while his hand reappeared and he placed a pile of small coins on the counter.

Sarah picked up the money and smiled at her friend. She and Laila were so desperate to get the swimming costumes and head off for a swim in the sea that they didn't think about counting the change.

"Thank you, Sir," said Sarah picking up her parcel.

"Thank you, Sir," said Laila doing likewise.

"Thank you, Ladies!" grinned the man, stuffing the note into his inside jacket pocket, "Very nice doing business with you! Please call again!"

"Mom! Mom!" yelled Sarah and Laila as they shot into the guest house overjoyed at their purchases.

"Shh!" replied Elisabeth, putting her finger to her lips, "Quiet! People are trying to nap you know!"

"Sorry," said Sarah, "Mom, we've got our costumes," she whispered, "I'll put the change on your bedside table, we're going to get changed and then go for a swim, OK?"

"Sure, OK, honey, but be careful and be back by five o'clock!"

Chapter 20

THE MEN'S CAMP

A train journey wasn't needed for Jacob, Terry and the rest of the men on the Rushen Castle when they arrived in Douglas because the camps they were to stay at were in the town itself.

Before they were moved off to their billets the men were made to gather around. There was a large crowd of locals watching the proceedings but they were kept at a safe distance by the police.

"Listen up!" yelled a man on a soapbox, "Listen up! LISTEN UP!"

Very quickly everyone was silent and looking at the man, who was wearing a three piece suit with a black tie. His hair was plastered down to his head and he had a well trimmed moustache.

"Can anyone understand or speak English?" called the man.

There was some muttering amongst the men but many were nodding in agreement.

"Very well. You will now march to the camp in a compact and orderly fashion." You could tell that the man was more used to speaking to soldiers than civilians as he really didn't know what to do to get them moving. To soldiers he would have just ordered 'quick march!' But there was no way the motley gathering assembled in front of him would respond to that, eventually he called out gingerly, "Now please get going! NOW!"

As the men were marched from the docks to their camps, they passed a newsagent's shop. Outside on the wall was a board with the headline from a local paper.

"The Isle of Man welcomes internees to its shore" was the headline from the local newspaper, the Mona's Herald, and it was in big bold black letters.

As they passed the poster Terry, ever the joker, reached across and pulled the poster off the board, and right there and then he ripped it up and started eating the pieces.

"Mm," he mumbled, his mouth full of paper, as some of the other men laughed, "it's a lot tastier than bread and butter."

"But not bread and butter with jam?" questioned Jacob chuckling.

"No, it could do with some jam! Strawberry, maybe!"

As they marched past, the paper shop owner came rushing out, waving his fist and shouting.

"Hey, has somebody seen my poster?" he yelled.

Everyone shook their heads and someone from the crowd shouted, "What poster?"

"Well it was here just a minute ago."

"I see no poster!" said an internee as he walked past.

"Must be ze vind!" added another.

The shop owner stuck his finger in his mouth then pulled it out and held it above his head to test the wind.

"There is no bloomin' wind at all today!"

A muffled chuckle went up from the group as it continued on.

"What's that they're carrying, Ernie?" asked one onlooker to another as they stood in the crowd curiously watching the internees march passed.

"What, Ethel?" Asked Ernie.

"That thing they're carrying in a box around their necks?" Replied Ethel.

The lady was referring to the box that contained the internees' individual gas mask. Gas masks weren't needed, and were never issued, on the Isle of Man because they rarely saw a German plane in the sky and they had never been gassed by the Luftwaffe.

"No idea, Ethel, maybe it's their sandwiches," replied Ernie.

"Oh, of course," muttered Ethel, "sandwiches!"

As the men marched on they passed houses where people seemed to be moving all their things out, as if they were moving house, but today all in the street were moving house at the same time!

As the marching men neared the bustling residents, they all stopped what they were doing and stared at the internees. Some of the people called out names at the marching group. Some raised their fists and threatened them. All of them looked sad and quite angry.

As Jacob neared one group of neighbours he couldn't resist asking them why they were moving out and why they were so angry towards the internees "Cos it's all your lot's fault!" said one woman angrily.

"What is?" Asked Jacob.

"Why we have to move out!"

"But I don't understand."

"We're having to move out, lad, because your lot are moving in!"

"Our lot?"

"Aye, you Germans."

"But I'm not German, I'm American!" protested Jacob, shouting over his shoulder "and I didn't *ask* to be brought here!"

"And we *certainly* didn't ask for you!" replied the woman bitterly.

The more he stared, the more empty houses Jacob could see as they marched along.

"They're nearly all empty," he muttered to Terry, who was still chewing, "have you not finished that paper yet, Terry?" "Naw," Terry spat the papier mache out and pulled a face, "Blah! Blah! Actually it's not that nice, I definitely prefer bread and butter!"

"With jam?" Laughed Jacob.

"Mmm of course...blah! Especially strawberry!" Chuckled Terry.

After what seemed like an endless march, the prisoners were split into groups and marched off in different directions.

"Please march along the rest of the promenade and across the swing bridge onto the Mooragh!" ordered the man in charge.

As they walked there were workmen busy building high fences all along the sea front. At the other side of the swing bridge there was a large barbed wire gate that was closed after Jacob's group had passed through it.

As Jacob and Terry's group marched on they could hear a wireless blaring out from one of the houses where the people were packing up the last of their possessions ready to move out.

"And now, the news at five pm. This is the BBC broadcasting from London...this afternoon the Prime Minister, Winston Churchill, has said that today be declared the Day of National Prayer for the Army. The Prime Minister has asked that all citizens join him, the Cabinet and His Majesty the King and pray for all of our brave men who are currently fighting the forces of Adolf Hitler in Northern France."

Chapter 21

DAY OF NATIONAL
PRAYER FOR THE ARMY

As the warm French spring afternoon approached evening the immense British Expeditionary Force army of almost four hundred thousand soldiers which had been in France since September 1939 was withdrawing as quickly as it could and keeping its fingers crossed for some luck!

A massive military pincer movement by the enemy was forcing the retreat. Two immense German armies flanked the British forces, pushing them further and further north until they had nowhere to go. To the east, moving in from the low countries of Belgium and Holland, was the huge army commanded by General Fedor von Bock. To the west, the awesome war machine commanded by General Gerd von Rundstedt was closing in from Paris. To make matters worse this pincer movement was added to by the rapidly approaching panzer tanks of Von Rundstedt which were now within ten miles of Dunkirk and the unstoppable force was moving steadily closer.

As they retreated, the British forces were hoping and praying for a miracle of monumental proportions.

Although not a religious man, twenty three year old Private Walter Simpkins was praying as hard as everyone else. Simpkins was from Port Erin on the Isle of Man and was part of the BEF that had made it to the vast open beaches of Dunkirk in northern France earlier that day. News and rumours had spread like wild fire amongst the soldiers who had set up their camp in the dunes along the miles of beautiful beach.

"They're almost here!" uttered Spike Gemmell, a young Scottish private from Dumfries and Galloway on the Scottish borders.

"How do you know that, Spike?" asked Walter who was sick and tired of listening to Spike moan. He'd been moaning for weeks now and Walter couldn't imagine why Spike had even bothered to sign up to be a soldier.

Even though he was young in years Walter had grown up very fast in the eight months he had been in France and one of his biggest lessons was to learn that everyone dealt with fear in different ways. Some men stayed quiet, really quiet, and wouldn't speak with anyone when they were frightened, others chattered nonstop, mostly talking gibberish. His mate Spike fell into the latter category, and he on the whole fell into the former, though he wasn't as bad as some.

"I can hear 'em, that's how."

"Hear them? Hear who?" asked Walter.

As British trucks and machinery moved towards the beach there was little peace and quiet.

"I can hear 'em, Wally! Them!"

"Who, Spike?"

"Them! The Panzers, I can hear their engines, I can you know!" Spike's eyes stared ahead, as if mesmerised by the sound of an impending evil.

The Panzers or Panzer Tank Divisions were developing a real reputation for brutal efficiency that scared their enemies to death. They had helped sweep the German armies to rapid success in their invasions of Poland, the Netherlands, Belgium and France, and parts of the Soviet Union in the past year and it seemed a sure fire bet that they would be crossing the channel before the year was out and trying to invade Britain.

The brave soldiers of the BEF, although frightened, had no doubt about what they would be facing in a very short space of time and they would fight to the very last ounce of their energy to defend their country.

To take his mind off the impending doom, Walter got a piece of paper out of his pocket and a pen and he started to write to his parents on the Isle of Man

"Dear Mum and Dad, I hope you're both keeping well and business is OK. Are there many visitors on the island still? I suppose not, I suppose the war has even got as far as Port Erin?

There are a couple of lads here from the island, not from Port Erin like, they're from Douglas, but still, it's nice to talk with people from the island.

My best mate is a lad called Spike, he's good company for the most part, but he doesn't half witter sometimes!

The weather has been good for the past few weeks, warm and sunny, I bet it's raining on the island, I really miss the rain. When it rains here it's normally part of a storm, not that fine rain that wets you through back home, but heavy stuff.

Anyway, I'm hoping to get some leave soon, so I'll be home probably before you get this letter.

> *Your loving son,*
> *Walter."*

Walter folder the paper and popped it into a grubby envelope before passing it to a friend taking some more mail to be posted.

Chapter 22

SWIMMING IN THE IRISH SEA

Hundreds of miles north-west of the fear and confusion that was raging amongst young British soldiers on a sunny afternoon on a beach in northern France, was a scene of blissful tranquillity on the southern tip of the Isle of Man.

"Mom! Mom! Come in! The water's really lovely!" yelled Sarah Becker as she swam with her new best friend.

Sarah and Laila were splashing each other and playing tag in the sea. The beach was quite crowded, as many of the women who had been sent to the Isle of Man enjoyed some peace, quiet and sunshine after the long journey from their homes. Around the coves, ladies sat and sunbathed, others who were less daring just walked slowly along the sea's edge and paddled, but some enjoyed a good, long swim. One lady, who seemed to be a really confident swimmer, set off at such a pace that a local policeman had to borrow a small fishing boat and go after her. When they caught up to her the lady claimed that she had lost track of where she was.

"Five more minutes!" shouted Elisabeth, "and then you need to come out, it's nearly time for tea!"

"OK!"

As Elisabeth Becker sat on the beautiful golden beach and watched the children giggling and shouting, her mind started drifting and she felt fear and heartache flow through her body once again.

Elisabeth knew that her husband was safe and sound and probably working hard trying to shorten the war in any way he could but where was her son? Her twelve year old boy, Jacob. She hoped he would be on the Isle of Man, at least that way he would be safe from German attack.

Chapter 23

JACOB'S CAMP

The men's camp at Mooragh in Douglas was about as different from the Rushen Camp at Port Erin and Port St Mary as it could be. From the start it was patently obvious that internees were to be treated more like prisoners than guests.

At the Mooragh there was none of the freedom that was afforded to the ladies in the south west of the Island, there was no visiting local shops because all of the shops within the boundaries of the camp had been cleared, there was no swimming in the Irish Sea because barbed wire fences had been put up to stop the men even getting on the beach and there was no friendly seaside landladies making salad and rhubarb crumble for lunch.

But the first group of detainees which included Terry and Jacob, got a very strong feeling that things were going to become worse, much worse, in the town as more detainees arrived.

The island's capital was a hive of activity. Almost the whole of Douglas was full of workmen, carpenters, builders, labourers and they were putting up miles upon miles of fences, they were adapting large buildings inland of the town, and commandeering more and more buildings.

It was becoming very apparent to everyone at the Mooragh camp that they were expecting a lot more people to arrive and be detained on the Isle of Man.

Jacob and Terry were billeted in a normal three bedroom house with another six men, two in each bedroom and two in the living room, which was now a makeshift bedroom.

The family who owned the house seemed to have left in a real hurry as they'd just taken what they could carry, so the beds, tables, chairs and cupboards were all still there.

No one was to use the kitchen by order of the police. Breakfast, lunch and dinner was to be served three hundred yards away in one of the seafront hotels. Breakfast would be at 8 am, lunch at 12 noon and tea at 5.30 pm.

"I hope they don't just serve bread and butter!" joked Terry.

"Why? What would you prefer, Terry? Newspaper maybe?" replied Jacob.

The rest of the men who were in their house could hear the boy's conversation and they all chuckled. Comedian Terry puffed up with pride as the men enjoyed a laugh. He quite liked the idea of being a joker, the trouble was, he was quite accident prone and his unintentional mishaps seemed to cause the most laughter! Even sober, Terry could trip over his own feet. Trying to walk down the gang plank of the Rushen Castle, he slipped, fell and rolled all the way down, nearly scuttling Jacob who was agile enough to leapfrog over Terry as he continued his undignified descent on to the dockside! Trying to pick himself up and look as if what had just took place hadn't really happened caused his fellow passengers even more amusement as he stood there brushing dirt from his dishevelled clothes!

It was now five o'clock as Terry and Jacob sat on their beds and waited for tea time to be called by a camp hooter.

"Tell me about America, Jake?" Terry sighed, like most people at that time he had never been abroad, in fact the furthest he had been was to the Isle of Man today. And now because he'd been on a boat over the sea he thought that he *was* abroad.

"Oh, Terry, you'd love America, man!"

"Would I?" Terry loved listening to Jacob speak.

"Sure! America's the best! Just the best! And best of all we've got baseball, basketball, football, popcorn and the prettiest girls in the world!" Jacob had become quite interested in girls over the past six months and he was sure that no girls could be as beautiful as the ones back in Concord.

"Mm..." thought Terry, pondering what Jacob had said, although girls interested him, he didn't interest them, "is baseball the one that's like rounders?" asked Terry not quite sure what baseball was.

"Well I suppose, but better, much better, I mean baseball is way better than cricket, I mean nothing ever happens in cricket, it goes on and on for days and for what? A split second of action? Now baseball, baseball's full of action, nonstop action."

"But they just wear their underwear?" sniggered Terry.

"Excuse me?" Jacob stared at Terry.

"Don't they wear long johns?"

"They're not long john's, Terry, they're pants! Special pants!"

"Well, I saw pictures of these pants in a magazine and they look a lot like the undies my dad wears, maybe a bit cleaner and definitely whiter but undies all the same."

"Are your dad's undies not very white then?" chuckled Jacob.

"White?" snorted Terry, a vivid image of his dad's underpants springing to mind, "White? I'll have you know that my dad's undies haven't been really white since 1925! And that's when he bought them!"

All the men in the house had a good laugh at the prospect of Terry's dad's grotty underpants.

"But getting back to baseball," continued Jacob as the laughter died down, "their pants are nothing like underpants, Terry, and definitely not like you dad's undies!"

Terrys company really made being in this place and in the middle of this nightmare a whole lot better. In fact, chatting with Terry frequently made Jacob forget, for a short time at least, that he had been cruelly separated from his family and did not have a clue where they were or if he would ever see them again. Jacob was really glad that his new friend was there with him.

"What about American football?" asked Terry.

"You mean football, it's not American football, it's just football."

"No, *we* play football, Jacob Becker, we kick a ball about, with our FEET! It's a beautiful game, and the best player in the whole world is Stanley Matthews!"

"No way! We play the real football," argued Jacob.

"And that's another game where you Americans insist on playing in your underpants!" laughed Terry.

"They're *special* pants, Terry, NOT UNDERWEAR," shouted Jacob

"Well, they look a lot like underpants to me, Becker!"

"Underpants! Thunderpants! You're crazy. You've got underpants on the brain, which is probably where yours should be, over your head to shut you up," Jacob patted Terry's head forcefully as if to emphasise the point.

Terry chuckled. "I suppose American popcorn is good though?" Terry licked his lips.

"Yeah, American popcorn is the best!" agreed Jacob just as the hooter sounded calling all the internees to their tea.

Chapter 24

THE RADAR NETWORK

Although Professor Carl Becker was staying in a very plush and luxurious place, being at Bawdsey Manor definitely was not a holiday for him. He knew that he had an important job to do, a job that he was determined to do to the very best of his ability and as quickly as he could so then he and his family could get on the first ship headed back across the Atlantic to the States.

As soon as he had been shown around the research facility, Carl rolled up his sleeves and got straight down to work.

The radar system was up and running efficiently and it had proved time and time again that it did provide Britain with an extra advantage over the Luftwaffe, it was a brilliant early warning system, an ear to the sky!

As soon as German planes got within range of the radar they were spotted and the RAF was able to scramble its fighters to head off the enemy. It also meant that the RAF was able to target its resources effectively so that, although they had fewer planes than the Luftwaffe, they could make sure they were in the right place at just the right time.

The British Government and Prime Minister, Winston Churchill, certainly knew the advantage that radar gave them against a vastly superior military power. The German Air Force had many more attack fighter planes than the RAF.

The mainstay of the Luftwaffe was the Messerschmitt Bf 109 which was a very advanced aircraft. It could fly at over one hundred miles per hour faster than the mainstay of the RAF the

Hawker Hurricane and whilst the Supermarine Spitfire was more than a match it was much harder and expensive to produce than the versatile Hurricane.

Many Hurricane pilots reported that the 109 pilots would use deadly tactics against them. Whilst the Hurricanes were flying along at their top speed, the 109's would zoom up to them from behind, above or below, fire off their guns and then speed off before the Hurricane pilot even knew what was happening!

Britain certainly needed radar and needed it networked in a failsafe way. Communications wizard Professor Carl Becker was the man who could help do just that.

Carl had to work within a small dedicated team that were wiring up the network of towers so if one was hit and put out of action, the direction of the signal from the other towers could be adjusted to compensate for the loss. That way there would be no gaps in the coverage.

"The team are waiting to meet you in the conference room," Professor Jim Wilson told Carl Becker as they finished their tour, "they're really excited!"

"Are they? Oh OK, right."

Wilson led Carl through the dark oak double doors into a large conference room, which was dominated by an immensely long oval table. There were about twenty scientists sat around the table and, as the two men entered the room, all eyes were on the newcomers.

Jim Wilson walked to the head of the table and bid Carl take the spare seat next to his.

"Good evening, everyone."

"Good evening," mumbled the crowd.

"Well, some of you have already bumped into him, but I suppose this is the formal part, ladies and gentlemen, may I introduce, from Massachusetts Institute of Technology, communications systems expert, Professor Carl Becker!"

There was a polite round of clapping as Professor Wilson bid Carl to take the floor.

"Err..." he mumbled, feeling a little embarrassed, "thank you very much, I would say it's nice to be back in England, I am English after all, but most of you who I've already spoken to will understand why I can't," Carl paused and took a deep breath to steady his nerves, "but whatever is happening with my family, I can assure you that I am one hundred and ten per cent committed to this project. I know that radar is vital to the war effort, vital to achieving victory over Germany, vital to making this war as short as possible. And that's something we all want!"

There was a round of applause.

"And I believe that effective networking of the system could be the crucial element of the project."

Again another round of applause.

"OK then, I think I'd like to get straight down to work on the potential flaws in the radar network. I'd like to start out with a brain storming exercise. I'm absolutely certain that we've got the most talented people with the best brains in the world in this room. So let's start putting them to work solving this problem..."

Chapter 25

DUNKIRK

As dusk started to fall on the huge, sandy beach at Dunkirk, the thousands of British soldiers were starting to imagine that the worst was going to happen.

For miles and miles, the endless dunes were full of makeshift camps. Tens of thousands of soldiers could almost feel the ground start to shake as the ruthless Panzer divisions closed in for the kill.

In a corridor of land about sixty miles long and fifteen to twenty five miles wide that bordered the English Channel, the immense withdrawing army was being squeezed harder and harder by the German forces.

But as the British Expeditionary Forces sat waiting for the end to come, for some reason the Germans stopped their advance. Many believe that Mother Nature had dealt a stroke of good luck for the soldiers and that the Germans had deemed the terrain around Dunkirk unsuitable for the heavy Panzer tanks and other armoured divisions to cross. Some people thought that Hitler was awaiting the arrival of more manpower so that the British could be totally wiped out, in other words, brutally annihilated. Yet some people had the ludicrous idea that the Fuhrer was trying to negotiate an eleventh hour truce with Winston Churchill.

Chapter 26

THE PHONE CALL

Affectionately known to the British people as Winnie, Winston Leonard Spencer-Churchill had only been the British Prime Minister for just over two weeks. He had become Prime Minister after Neville Chamberlain had resigned on May 10th and recommended he take over the job.

Instantly recognisable, with his portly appearance, round face and ever present cigar, Churchill had, up until now, a varied political and military career, serving as the First Sea Lord of the Navy, experiencing life in the trenches of the First World War as a commanding officer and then serving his country in numerous Cabinet roles.

You could say that Winston Churchill's first days in charge of Great Britain was truly a baptism of fire and this evening would be one of the most surreal and unexpected of his entire premiership.

The Prime Minister had just finished a private, light dinner with his trusted bodyguard, Detective Inspector Walter Henry Thompson, and was sat lighting up another of his trademark cigars when the door quietly opened and a young male clerk poked his head around it and coughed lightly.

"No need to cough man, I do know you're there," said the Prime Minister without turning around. Churchill had sensed movement in his dining partner, the ever vigilant Thompson, a man who stuck to his charge like an insect to fly paper.

"Yes of course, sorry," replied the clerk feeling somewhat embarrassed, "excuse me, Prime Minister."

"Well? What is it?" replied Churchill drawing deeply on the Cuban cigar and puffing out a cloud of smoke. He still didn't turned around.

"There's a telephone call for you, Sir."

"Telephone? Well, who is it man?"

"Err..." the clerk didn't quite know what to say.

"Well, man! Spit it out!" The Prime Minister couldn't abide people who didn't get straight to the point, "I don't bite!" This wasn't altogether true, Churchill could be fearsome.

"Err..."

"SPEAK!"

"It's Adolf Hitler on the line," blurted out the clerk preparing himself for the fallout of the declaration.

"WHAT?" The cigar dropped out of Churchill's mouth and would have fallen to the ground had it not been for the lightening quick reactions of the completely reliable Detective Inspector Thompson who swooped down and caught the expensive Havana then juggled it from hand to hand to avoid burning himself!

"He says it's Adolf Hitler."

"Has security checked this?" asked the PM.

"Yes, Sir, he's passed all the security checks, they think it is actually him!"

"Very well!" replied Churchill, getting to his feet, glancing at Thompson, "What do you think, Wally?"

"Interesting, Sir, very interesting," replied the man of few words.

"Precisely."

Winston Churchill's large, rotund form barged out of the sitting room and through to his private study, at once summoning for a translator. Translators were always on duty twenty four hours a day should Germany either need to be contacted or try to contact the British Government.

As the Prime Minister made his way to the study the quietly assured Thompson, as always, stayed within touching distance of his chief. Detective Inspector Thompson never left the Prime Minister's side, never.

Churchill and Thompson started their association in 1921 but when Winnie had assumed a more low profile role the ex detective retired to become a grocer. It was only on 22 August 1939 when Churchill sent Thompson an urgent and mysterious telegram reading "Meet me, Croydon Airport, 4.30pm, Wednesday," did he resume his responsibilities.

At the time of the telegram Winston Churchill had been sent intelligence reports that his life was in danger from assassination attempts by groups including the Nazis. Churchill realised only one man could be relied upon to offer the total protection he needed.

The red faced translator arrived, puffing and panting from the exertion of running across Whitehall, just as Churchill reached his desk, sat down and picked up the phone. The PM impatiently beckoned the translator to pick up the other phone on the desk and sit down. Calmly and quickly, Thompson grabbed another receiver but remained standing a few feet away.

"Hello?" said Churchill into the receiver.

The translator quickly repeated the word in German.

"Good evening, Prime Minister," came the unmistakeable voice of the Fuhrer in German.

Churchill stared at Thompson who nodded. He knew that Winnie was speaking to Adolf Hitler.

The translator quickly pressed the record button on his phone.

"Good evening, Herr Hitler, I must say this is an unexpected pleasure," Churchill was completely charming and so very English.

"Is it really so unexpected, Prime Minister?" asked the German Chancellor.

"Sorry?"

"Unexpected? You say that my call to you is unexpected? On this, the day you have called your day of national prayer."

Churchill wasn't at all surprised that Hitler was totally abreast of what was happening in Britain, as Germany, like Britain, had spies everywhere.

"Let us not waste time with games, Chancellor," replied Churchill firmly, getting straight down to business.

"Very well, Prime Minister, as you wish." The Fuhrer paused briefly, "the reason for my call is that I know you are fully aware of how futile the resistance of the British Expeditionary Force is."

"Do you?" replied Winnie.

"May I remind you, Sir, that as we speak over three hundred thousand of your men are trapped in a narrow corridor of land about sixty miles long and twenty miles wide in northern France. They are surrounded by two of my supremely well trained and equipped armies and my Panzer division is closing in on them."

"Ah."

"Ah indeed!" cackled Hitler, the laugh sending a shiver down Winnie's spine, "they are trapped, Prime Minister, in a trap I myself laid and do you know what will happen next?"

"Enlighten me," sighed the Prime Minister.

"I am about to tighten the noose around their necks and then I will start to squeeze."

"What do you want, Herr Hitler?" Churchill didn't want to listen to a rant by the mad man, but he did know that the mark of a really gifted tactician was to turn adversity to their own advantage and he knew Hitler's thoughts could easily be blinded by the glorious prospect of victory.

"Prime Minister, I am calling to ask for your surrender!" It was Herr Hitler who came straight to the point this time.

Winston Churchill was silent for a couple of moments.

"Prime Minister? Prime Minister, are you still there?" asked the Fuhrer.

"Yes, Herr Hitler, I'm still here," replied Winnie slowly as he worked through everything methodically in his head.

This could prove to be an opportunity that even I hadn't foreseen! Thought the Prime Minister.

Who could have predicted that the Fuhrer himself would call Churchill by telephone on tonight of all nights? As hundreds of thousands of British troops remained stranded on the French beaches at the total mercy of the vastly superior German forces, Winston Churchill was being thrown a lifeline by the Fuhrer himself! This was like a gift from heaven!

Straight away Churchill knew what he had to say, knew what he had to do.

Stall the Germans! Make time! Give our boys a chance!

Winston Churchill had to stall Hitler's advance, hold up the German military action and buy time. By any means at his disposal the Prime Minister had to use this once in a lifetime opportunity to buy his armies vital time.

"I need to think about this," mumbled Churchill quietly as if to imply defeat.

"You have forty eight hours!" replied Hitler slamming the phone down furiously.

"I think Herr Hitler has just thrown our boys a lifeline, Wally!" sighed the PM reaching for his cigar.

Half a smile crossed Walter's face in response.

Chapter 27

TROUBLE AT THE MEN'S CAMP

It must have been just after midnight when Jacob was roughly roused from his deep slumber. He hadn't slept properly for two days so he felt absolutely exhausted and away to the world. He was in such a deep sleep that his body refused to stir when someone started to vigorously shake him awake.

"Jake! Jake!" A voice from far away was calling Jacob's name, it was a familiar voice.

"No, Dad, it can't be morning yet!" moaned Jacob. "Go away!" he protested, refusing to open his eyes, "I'm still tired!"

"Jake! Jake!" The voice wouldn't let up, it was calling louder.

"Yeah, what? What is it?" mumbled Jacob as he slowly came round but still refused to open his eyes.

"Jake, wake up, Jake, there's something going on outside!" whispered Terry, "Come and look."

When Jacob wrenched himself from his slumber he saw that Terry was stood up and standing peering out of the window. It was still pitch black outside.

"What time is it?" Jacob asked

"Dunno," replied Terry in barely more than a whisper.

"What are you doing, Terry," mumbled Jacob, sitting up in bed.

"Sh!!" whispered Terry, "I'm watching."

"Watching what?"

"I'm watching what's going on outside. Quick, Jake, come here! Come and look! Quick!"

Reluctantly, Jacob threw back his bed covers and walked over to join Terry by the window. Jacob peered sleepily in disbelief.

Outside were about half a dozen men, internees, and probably internees that were Jewish refugees from Germany or other parts of Europe by the look of their dishevelled clothing. They looked like they had been travelling for weeks or even months before their journey over to the Isle of Man and hadn't changed their clothes in all that time.

As Jacob and Terry looked on in amazement they saw that the men were in varying stages of trying to escape from the camp. Some men were just starting to clamber onto the fence, some had scaled high up it, risking being cut to shreds by the barbed wire that topped it and were making their way down the beach towards the sea. And they could just make out the swaying figure of a man who was actually already in the dark, menacing looking sea wading out into the pitch black waves in the direction of the English mainland.

"Hey!" called a guard who was running towards the fence, "Stop! Stop now!"

Suddenly, powerful blazing spotlights were switched on shining bright white lights swamped the fence. They were swarming all over the men who lifted their hands off the fence to shield their eyes.

"Stop!" called another guard, "Stop or we'll shoot!"

But the warning didn't stop the desperate men, who were determined to get away at any cost.

Jacob knew that no one he'd spoken to on his journey had wanted to be interned in the camp, he certainly didn't want to be here and neither did Terry, but nobody had seemed to be so desperate as to try and escape and risk being shot at or drowned.

As they peered someone burst into their bedroom. Startled, Jacob and Terry span around, and then let out a sigh of relief. It was only one of their housemates, Wolfgang Henkell.

Wolfgang was a German Jewish refugee, but he had travelled to England with a few other people that he knew. His family were wealthy and had connections all across Europe.

Wolfgang was a musician by trade, he played the piano in a large world famous orchestra in Munich and had travelled the world before the war. Although really scruffy at the moment with long shaggy black hair, and a thick black moustache and beard, he said he was normally very clean cut, he said he had to be to play in a prestigious orchestra like the Munich Philharmonic where they insisted that a man's hair could not be allowed to grow any longer than his collar.

"Hey! Have you seen what's happening?" whispered Wolfgang excitedly in good English as he joined the boys at the window and peered out.

"Yeah," replied Terry, whose gaze had returned to the escape.

"I wonder why they're trying to escape," said Jacob, rubbing his sleepy eyes.

"Why?" asked Wolfgang

"Yeah, I'm mean it's so risky."

"Why? Because they're scared, Jacob," declared Wolfgang, "scared and desperate, that's why!"

"Stop or I'll shoot!" shouted a guard again as the men kept on going, "FINAL WARNING!"

The nearest of the escaping prisoners didn't stop so the guard raised his rifle and aimed into the sky. He quickly fired off two rounds.

BANG! BANG!

The darkness of the night seemed to muffle sounds but the cracks from the rifle sounded like sharp violent claps of thunder, and they were deafeningly loud.

Inside the house Jacob, Terry and Wolfgang all jumped at the sudden noise. Frozen with fear, they held their breath.

At the sound of the gunshots a couple of men who had just started to climb the fence stopped their ascent and dropped to the ground where they lay face down in on the shore completely motionless, except for their hands waving as a sign of surrender.

A man who was right at the top and about to go over stopped and started slowly untangling himself from the barbed wire, then he carefully climbed down the fence and ran to the other two on the ground and joined them facedown.

But the two men who had made it over the fence and were running towards the sea continued running defiantly towards the water.

BANG! BANG! BANG! Another guard fired three more shots that thundered into the dark night.

BANG! BANG! BANG! Three more shots.

The men on the beach fell on to the sand, afraid to move a single muscle in case the next bullet was meant to kill them.

"I think that's all of them," declared Jacob turning around, relieved that no one had died.

"Is it?" asked Terry, still staring.

"No, it's not," said Wolfgang pushing past the boys to get a better look, "there's another one, the one in the water remember, look you can just see him swimming out to sea!" Wolfgang was pointing and the boys following his direction, could just about make out a dark object bobbing around in the water. As they watched, a couple of spotlight beams found the man and started following him.

The sound of boat engines throbbed across the night air.

The boys watched as the head turned around and the man stopped swimming. As he stopped he suddenly seemed to lose all his energy, his muscles probably sapped by the cold spring water of the Irish Sea and the exertion of the swim. As everyone watched, the man suddenly started waving his hands about, a pathetic cry of help reached over the noise of engines as the swimmer appeared to lose any last drop of strength, his head disappearing under the waves.

"He's in trouble," cried Jacob, "I know he is."

"Yeah, he looked tired," agreed Terry.

Even as Terry spoke the man came up again and everyone breathed a sigh of relief. Yet their relief was short lived as he went under again only to bob up again a few seconds later. The man was struggling now and as the boat got closer and closer he went under for a third and final time.

As the boat got within a few yards of where the man had gone under a policeman bravely pulled off his jacket and dived into the sea. He swam over to the spot where the man had been and dived under, his legs kicking out of the water to propel him under.

Everyone waited and prayed. The policeman came up for air and shouted something at the boat then he dived again.

Another policeman peeled off his jacket and helmet and dived over to help his colleague.

After a minute or so they both bobbed up again this time they were struggling to pull something heavy between them back to the boat. The policemen heaved the motionless body towards the boat and strong hands reached overboard and pulled the prisoner out. Then they reached back for the two exhausted policeman.

Shouts echoed from the small boat amid a couple of minutes of frantic activity and then silence. No noise, no movement, nothing, just silence, total eerie silence as the boat bobbed gently on the cold water.

"He's dead," said Wolfgang in nothing more than a whisper.

"What?" said Jacob, turning around to stare at his friend, "Dead?"

"He's drowned," Wolfgang was certain of it.

"How do you know?" asked Terry.

"They tried to save him, probably gave him the kiss of life and chest massage, I've done it myself, but they've all stopped now, see, there's no movement on that boat, none at all. He was under for too long, almost five minutes by my reckoning, no one can stay under for five minutes and live, it's not humanly possible. No, I'm sure he's drowned."

Slowly, the boat turned and started heading back to the port. At the fence the escapees were made to stand up and were handcuffed by the guards before being marched off at gunpoint.

"What I don't understand," said Jacob quietly as the spotlights were switched off, and the blanket of silent darkness returned, "is why they would want to risk trying to escape, I mean, it must be over fifty miles to the mainland, you wouldn't stand a chance of swimming it!"

"No," agreed Terry, "and I bet the water's freezing cold."

"Yeah," agreed Jacob, "it's pointless."

"Pointless to you maybe, Jacob, but they're obviously terrified," whispered Wolfgang very quietly as if he was making doubly sure that no one was listening to what he was saying, "really, really scared."

"Of what?" asked Jacob.

"Of the Nazis," replied Wolfgang, who spoke the word with real hatred in his voice, while at the same time looking over his shoulder at the door. There was nobody there, there were no Nazis in their house. But even he was frighteneed.

"Of the Nazis?" repeated a disbelieving Jacob, "but Wolfgang, the Nazis are in Europe, in Germany, not in England and definitely not on the Isle of Man. I think we'd know if they were here!"

"Yeah!" agreed Terry.

Jacob and Terry had a youthful confidence that Wolfgang had grown out of years before.

"They are though, my friends, they are," he muttered in a weary voice, "there are Nazis in this camp and they're mixed in with Jews and, believe me, there's a lot of fear about."

"How come they're mixed in with Jews?" asked Jacob.

"Because it's chaos here Jacob, you can see that, nobody really prepared the people on this island for us, nobody prepared the camps properly, I mean you can see they're still putting the fences up! And there have been mistakes made, terrible mistakes that have cost that poor soul his life." Wolfgang paused, as if as a sign of respect for the drowned man, and then continued in nothing more than a whisper, "It's not easy for you two I know, you're not German, sure you have German family, but you're not German. You're American," he said looking at Jacob, "and you're English," he looked at Terry, "you don't know what it's like back home. You see, the Nazis hate Jews, I mean really hate us. They want to kill us all, murder every last one of us, men, women and even children! In fact they want to wipe us from history. And I bet that those men who tried to escape have been threatened, and not just them, I imagine they threatened their families back home too."

"Threatened?" asked Terry.

"Well, something must have really scared them, Terry, if they would risk drowning out there like that desperate man. And do you know what?"

"What?" said Jacob.

"England is only separated from being invaded by the Nazis by a small stretch of water not even twenty miles wide."

As Wolfgang got up to go back to his bed the seriousness of the whole internment situation and the war in general suddenly dawned on poor Jacob and Terry. These two boys who had become close friends had just got caught up in the whole mess of the war, caught up, like Wolfgang had said, because members of their families happened to be born in Germany. But they weren't German at all. They couldn't imagine what it was like for a Jewish person living in Nazi Germany, not in a million years.

As he climbed into bed, Terry whispered to Jacob, "Do you think we'll be next, Jacob, Britain I mean."

It wasn't a question Jacob wanted to answer, in his heart he thought there was no way Germany could invade Britain, but in his head...

Chapter 28

GERTRUDE'S LIFE CHANGES

Thirty five year old mum of one, Gertrude Levy, had very similar features to those of her precious daughter. In fact had Gertrude not been more than twenty five years older than Laila you could safely have guessed that they were sisters.

Like her daughter, Gertrude had beautiful fair skin with a rosy complexion. She never wore make-up apart from a little rouge on her lips and her long brown hair, which was nearly down to her waist, was usually piled up on the top of her head in a neat bun.

Her husband, Ahren, a slim, plain looking, mousy haired man with a very pale complexion, was from a very well respected family of Berlin bankers and was totally devoted to both his career and his family.

They and their only child, Laila, lived in the wealthy residential Prenzlauer Berg part of central Berlin which lay just to the North East of neighbouring Mitte or midtown of the German capital.

The Levy's house was large, not palatial, but definitely substantial. It was a white painted, one hundred year old, terraced town house, with four storeys and marble columns on either side of the front door.

The family were so rich that they even had servants, two maids, a butler, a nanny and a cook. The staff lived on the very top floor of the house and each had their own room.

Because of all the domestic help, in all her years of being married to Ahren, Gertrude Levy had never had to lift a finger around the house, she didn't cook and she definitely didn't clean. So she could spend all her time, when she wasn't enjoying her daughter's company, organising parties and soirees for friends and her husband's business associates.

Gertrude's parties were legendary around Prenzlauer Berg. In the summer they were held in the large rear garden and when the weather wasn't too good, they were held in the living rooms on the ground floor of the house which could easily accommodate over a hundred people in comfort.

Gertrude's parties were nearly always themed, as a youngster she had always loved dressing up.

Just before the Nazis came to power, Gertrude threw her best party ever, a Roman themed party. Everyone dressed up as Romans! Some of the men wore togas, others dressed up as centurions with shiny metal armour and swords, some came as gladiators and slaves. They ate Roman food whilst they laid about on the floor on plump pillows and cushions! But since the Nazis came to power there had been no parties. In fact no one had felt much like partying, not with the prospect of what the Fuhrer, Adolf Hitler, might do to the Jews.

Gertrude Levy's life had changed beyond recognition. As soon as Hitler forced his way to power on a propaganda tide of bitterness, hate and envy, Gertrude's life changed very much for the worse. Anyone that didn't meet the little man's ideals was cast aside or worse, put in prison. And Jewish people seemed to have the worst treatment of all.

From the beginning of his reign of terror many Jews heard awful rumours that Adolf Hitler and his henchmen had formed horrendous plans for dealing with people of the Jewish faith, and other groups including gypsies and Jehovah Witness's. The rumours suggested that the Nazis wanted to put anyone who was a Jew in prison and throw away the key. But nobody in their wildest dreams could have predicted that Hitler would do what he did.

For more than six months before nine year old Laila actually left on the Kinderstransport for London, Gertrude and Ahren had discussed and made careful plans for their daughter. A friend of a friend apparently knew a single German woman in London, a woman who was reliable in the most important way, she needed money! The Levy's were told that Mrs Friedrich always needed money because she didn't like to work and her husband had left her with a big house to take care of. As they had plenty of money they could pay this Mrs Friedrich a more than generous allowance to make sure that she looked after their daughter properly. They decided that they would pay the allowance regularly and they would give her bonuses and rises just to make sure she kept on looking after Laila, just in case the war dragged on and on and something untoward happened to them! There would be ample funds to last until Laila reached eighteen and then a she would be able to control her own substantial finances.

When the plans were finally in place, Ahren wrote to a German banker friend who lived and worked in the city of London and arranged for the stipend for Mrs Friedrich to be organised. Monies were transferred to London and Mrs Friedrich was visited and vetted thoroughly by a close family friend who was passing through London on the way to America. Finally, everything was in place.

For almost a week before the day of Laila's departure, Gertrude cried almost nonstop. The 19th June 1939 was a very dark day indeed for the Levy family and for many other German Jewish families as they reluctantly bid a sorrowful farewell to their children. The families were sending their offspring to stay with strangers in faraway England not knowing if they would ever see them again.

The journey for Laila was a long one, lasting almost two days. It took her from Germany to Holland and from the Hook of Holland the children took a ferry to Harwich in England. Here they boarded a train for Liverpool Street Station in London.

There were many people of the Quaker faith running the Kinderstransport and the Levy's were so grateful to these kind, brave, selfless and committed people who, even though they weren't Jews, risked their lives to take Jewish children to safety.

But Laila's long journey was nothing compared to the one that her mother would soon be taking.

As soon as her baby had departed, the tearful Gertrude redoubled her determination for her and Ahren to also flee Germany. She couldn't bear to be apart from her daughter, and the situation in Berlin was rapidly becoming very serious indeed for Jews.

Gertrude wrote an emotional letter almost as soon as she stepped back through the door, tears streaming down her cheeks after taking her daughter to the station, and told her that she could expect to see her parents in less than one month's time, that they were leaving Germany and they had found a house in England, in the countryside well away from danger. She told her daughter that very soon they would all be a family again, happy and safe.

The Levy's comfortable suburban life changed beyond all recognition on the 25th June 1939. The day before their D-day, they received a short letter from Laila telling them that she had arrived in London, that she was settling in with Mrs Friedrich, who although a little odd was very nice, that she was pleased to get her mother's letter and that she was really looking forward to seeing them again soon.

All was normal that morning as Ahren got up as usual very early to go into the office. He always rose at five thirty so that he could be at his desk by seven. His commitment to his work was well known and respected. But as a dedicated wife Gertrude always rose with her husband so that they could eat breakfast and start the day together.

"Mr Ahren! Mr Ahren! Oh, Mr Ahren!" Cook was in a terrible state as she flew into the dining room that morning. Her fat face was bright purple and she was puffing like a steam engine.

"What is it, Marta?" asked Ahren calmly.

"Oh, Mr Ahren! Mr Ahren!" Marta could barely get her breath, and had to sit down for a few seconds.

123

"Now you take a deep breath, Marta, in...out...in...out, you know what happens when you don't breathe!"

"Yes, yes, Mr Ahren, I know," Marta's plump face was now back to a normal pink colour instead of the deep purple it had been a moment earlier.

"Now, are you OK?" He asked her calmly.

"Yes, Mr Ahren."

"Then please tell us what is wrong."

"There is trouble coming to this house!" said Marta dramatically. She often exaggerated so the Levy's weren't overly perturbed to begin with.

"What do you mean?" asked Gertrude sipping her coffee.

"What kind of trouble?" asked Ahren, wiping his mouth with his napkin and giving the cook his full attention.

"The cook from next door has just called in on her way to work in such a panic," started Marta, "she told me that she's seen police calling at houses all around lower Prenzlauer Berg, taking people away!"

"What do you mean taking people away, Marta?" Ahren was immediately uneasy, he had heard rumours at his gentleman's club of police calling at Jewish homes early in the morning and arresting families without giving any reason.

"All I know is what she told me, Mr Ahren, she said she saw police taking families out of their houses while they were still wearing their night clothes...making them get in vans...driving them away."

"Did she say if she knew who the families were, Marta?" asked Gertrude.

"No, she didn't know their names, Mrs Levy, but she did know that they were Jewish families."

Marta wasn't a Jew herself but as she had worked for the Levy's for more than fifteen years she felt like a member of the family and was totally dedicated to them.

"All of them?" asked Ahren, trying to clarify things.

"Yes, Mr Ahren, all of them, every single one."

When Marta left the room Ahren got up and started pacing up and down. He looked at his watch, it was almost six o'clock.

"It's starting isn't it?" asked Gertrude.

"Yes, Gerty, I fear it is."

Ahren and Gertrude, along with many other Jewish people, had feared that something like this might happen but they had hoped beyond hope that it wouldn't.

But the Levy's had made plans. As they told Laila, they had rented a house in south west England and transferred much of their money across to the London branch of the bank. Through a friend who was a lawyer they had obtained forged papers and passports that gave them new, non-Jewish identities, and they hoped that this would allow them to leave Germany more easily.

To aid their escape Ahren had rented a small house in a quiet neighbourhood of Berlin on the western edge of the city. They'd planned that this would act as a place where they could prepare for their journey and they had bought a brand new car and kept it in the garage. The car was always fully fuelled and ready to go.

Over the last few months the Levi's had carefully taken their things over to the house in the suburbs bit by bit and packed the car ready for a quick escape.

Another acquaintance, who owned a shipping business, had arranged a meeting with a contact who was the owner of a small cargo ship. After large sums of money had changed hands the man was eventually prepared to take the risk of taking the Levy's to England. So when the time was right to move, all that Ahren and Gertrude had to do was drive the 450 miles from Berlin to the Hook of Holland to where the boat was moored. But neither of them thought that a drive such as this would be easy, not easy at all.

"We must make our way to the house separately," said Ahren gravely as he helped his wife gather the last of her personal possessions into a small bag.

"Must we?" she replied, looking deep into his eyes. She had feared he would say this, "Must we really?"

Please say no, please say no! She thought, but she knew his answer and his reasoning behind it.

"Yes, we must. I'm sorry, Gerty, but you have to go directly to the house on your own, I suggest that you borrow one of Marta's old coats and hats then you won't look like a wealthy Jewish banker's wife, and I will go to the bank as normal so as to arouse as little suspicion as possible. We need to buy ourselves as much time as we can. It is vitally important."

"Oh, must you go into the bank, today of all days?" pleaded Gertrude .

"Yes, my dear, I must, I have some loose ends to tie up, but don't worry, it won't take me long. I should be finished and at the house just after lunch, we can get some rest and then at nightfall we will leave and drive to the coast."

As planned, Ahren left for work by the front door and Gertrude for the house in the suburbs by the back door. As he closed his front door for the final time Ahren glanced up and down the road.

Thank goodness, he thought. All was normal, the street was quiet with most of the residents still asleep in their beds, it was still early and there was no sign of any police.

Good, thought Ahren, *at least we have some time to get away. Time is good.*

As she walked, Gertrude was constantly looking over her shoulder to see if she was being followed, but she saw no one. She dare not risk taking public transport to get to the house, she knew that they were often searched by the Gestapo, the German police, and Jewish people were often singled out and removed for questioning even when they had done nothing wrong.

So Gertrude set off and walked the twelve long miles from their home in the city centre to the house.

Arriving just before lunch time she ate some fruit and drank just water as she sat peering through the window waiting for the arrival of her husband.

The afternoon was the longest of her entire life. One o'clock came and went but there was no sign of Ahren. Two o'clock, and still no sign of him. Three came and four and now Gertrude was starting to become very worried, anxiety coursing its way through her body.

Where could he be? Gertrude thought, as she watched people come and go along the quiet street. *Something must be wrong.*

At one point, a Gestapo vehicle drove slowly along the leafy road, the officers seemed to be scanning from side to side as if they were looking for something, or someone. Gertrude quickly moved away from the window and prayed like she had never prayed before.

Pease drive on! Please drive on!

And thankfully her prayers were answered, for when she dared to look out of the window again the car had vanished.

Just as light rain started to come down more heavily, shortly before four thirty, a tall man in a raincoat and with a hat pulled right down walked quickly along the street in the direction of the house. But instead of walking past like everyone else had done he stopped and turned, to her horror he walked up the short flight of steps and up to the front door of Gertrude's house.

Confused, Gertrude ducked down low so the man wouldn't see her. There was a light rap on the front door followed by a whisper.

"Gertrude, it's me!" called the man, "Gertrude!"

She recognised the voice straight away, "Johan?" she called back.

"Yes, let me in will you? Quickly!"

Gertrude scuttled around to the front hall and quickly opened the door just enough for Johan Bernstein to squeeze through.

"Johan, what are you doing here?" Gertrude didn't understand.

Johan had a worried look on his face.

Johan Bernstein was Ahren Levy's best friend. They had been friends ever since they were children. Their parents' houses were right next door to each other in the Berlin suburbs so the boys, neither of whom had brothers, played together like they were close family. And although Johan had never married, the Levy family often included him in the family things that they were doing, they invited him to their house for special occasion, for Honika, for birthdays and for other celebrations and they were happy to let him call in whenever he wanted.

"Johan, what is it? Where's Ahren?" asked the increasingly worried Gertrude.

"Ahren's been arrested," blurted Johan, clearly distressed.

"Arrested? When?"

"This morning."

"Where?"

"At the bank," Johan also worked at the city centre bank but didn't hold as senior a position as his friend. Johan was chief cashier.

"At the bank?" Gertrude couldn't quite believe what she was hearing, "but I thought the bank was as safe as houses? Ahren said so! I mean, it doesn't just have Jewish customers! Lots of other people bank with it!"

"Nothing Jewish is as safe as houses anymore, Gerty." Johan took off his dripping wet hat and placed it over the bottom of the staircase banister to dry. Gertrude then helped him off with his raincoat. Like Ahren, the other senior staff at the bank had long worried about the consequences for their firm with the Nazis being in power because as a respectable bank they took the preservation of the property and money of their customers very seriously indeed. Plans were made a long time ago that spanned the entire Atlantic Ocean. These plans involved much help from very good friends high up in the British, Canadian and United States Governments.

Over many months people from the United States had been visiting the bank and removing valuable goods and articles for shipping to North America on American boats. Because the United States was not at war with Germany the powers that be in Berlin had no right or power to stop the officials or the boats.

"Tell me what happened," Gertrude slowly walked to the kitchen. Johan sighed and wandered into the kitchen where he helped himself to a glass of water.

"It all happened so quickly, Gerty," he said sitting down at the kitchen table. It was all he could do to stop himself from shaking he was so shocked.

Gertrude sat opposite Johan, clasping her hands together on the table, desperate for answers.

"Just before the bank opened at ten o'clock there were people banging on the doors. As I said everything happened so quickly I don't know how Ahren managed to react so fast, he was amazing." Johan took a long drink, "as soon as they came, he appeared in the foyer and took me to one side. He said he wanted me to go with him, urgently. He escorted me down to the basement. You know there are lots of passageways under the building that very few people know about, even I didn't know about these! Anyway, Ahren gave me an old map and told me that I had to get my things from my apartment and then come and meet with you here."

"But why didn't he come himself?"

"Because he said it would make the police suspicious and that could put you in danger."

Gertrude's eyes were filling with tears now, as she clutched her hand over her mouth.

"Please don't cry, Gerty," pleaded Johan before continuing, he loved Gertrude like a sister, "Ahren said that as a board member he would be on the police's special list. If he was missing then it would arouse too much suspicion. They would come and look for him at the house."

"But..."

"He said that he thought being a board member might afford him some kind of protection, you know, political protection. He said that the board still had influence with the government."

"Well, I'm going to be with him!" said a determined Gertrude standing up from her chair.

"Sit down, Gerty," said Johan getting up and putting his hands gently on her shoulders, "please. If you go to the bank you'll be arrested and you will have no protection."

"But I'm Ahren's wife!" Argued Gertrude.

"But you're not a board member on one of Berlin's biggest banks!"

"You don't understand, I've got to be with him, I'm his wife, it's my place!"

"You're place is to be with your daughter!" snapped Johan.

There was an uncomfortable silence for a few moments as the events started to sink in.

"You said Ahren told you to get your things," said Gertrude, breaking the silence.

"Yes, he told me I was to collect some things, personal items from my place and then to come here and take you to England."

"You! I can't go with you to England! I can't leave Ahren here!"

"Look, Gerty," said Johan raising his voice, he was losing patience now, "I don't think you understand how serious all this is!"

Gertrude looked shocked and sat back down, staring at Johan. In all the time she'd know him he'd never spoken to her like this before.

"You don't know everything, Gerty! There's something else. When Ahren told me to go and get my things from my apartment I did, I went straight there, just as he'd asked, but I couldn't get in because when I got there the police were already there, evidently they're arresting any Jews that are connected with the bank, ANY Jews" Johan got up from the table, "they're searching for us right now, so, the plans have had to change."

"Change?"

"Yes, we're going to have to leave straight away."

"What, not wait until night fall? Won't that be risky?"

"It's the lesser of two evils, Gerty! If we stay we're going to be arrested very soon, maybe in the next hour or so. At least if we set off we might just stand a chance," as Johan spoke he was trying to convince himself as well as Gertrude that there was hope.

At four forty five, the large brand new black Mercedes-Benz W136 car with specially purchased number plates with the letters POL, to signify police, at the beginning roared out of the garage and headed west away from Berlin and towards the Hook of Holland. Ahren had bought the plates especially and thought they might allow the car a freer passage out of Berlin if they were approached.

Little did either Johan or Gertrude know that it wouldn't take them a day to get to the coast, nor a week, not even a month. Their journey would take them almost a year.

Chapter 29

THE DUNKIRK EVACUATION

After the German bombing the docks at the port of Dunkirk in northern France were far too badly damaged to be used for any British ships to moor up and allow members of the British Expeditionary Force to board them. So Captain William Tennant, the man in charge of the emergency evacuation, had the unenviable task of thinking of another way to get enough ships and boats to the shore fast enough to get over three hundred thousand men out of France!

"As you can see, Sir," said the chief engineer to Tennant as they surveyed the possibilities at the harbour, "there's just no way we can get any ships or boats into the harbour now, it's too badly damaged. The bombing's been too heavy."

"Mm," replied Tennant thoughtfully, staring at the harbour, before leaping up. Tenant was a man of actions and if there was anyone who could do this it was him, "I'm just going to take a look at the moles on either side, Sergeant, care to accompany me?"

"You're going over the harbour walls, Sir?" The sergeant's eyes widened.

"Precisely!" said the Captain, jumping over some rubble, and striding off, "If we can make it then so can everyone else!"

"But.. but...,Sir," stuttered the Sergeant as Tennant disappeared along the top of the harbour walls, stopping periodically to shift or move rubble, "we don't know if it's safe, Sir!"

"Safe?" yelled back Tennant, "Safe?"

"Yes, Sir."

"How safe do you think we'll all be, man, if we stay and wait for Jerry to arrive?"

When Captain Tennant inspected the harbour he was pleased to discover that not all of the Dunkirk sea front was unusable, in fact a lot of it was still intact and very strong. The two sea walls, known as the East and West Moles, which protected the harbour entrance from the open sea, were still in one piece and the water there was deep enough for even large ships to moor up against and the men could easily get along the harbour walls to the vessels.

With the outer Moles still intact the immense evacuation of the British Expeditionary Force began at dawn on the 27th May 1940 and on the 31st May, Private Walter Simpkins was overjoyed to see a ship flying the Manx flag approach the Eastern Mole where his division had been waiting for days.

"Spike! Spike!" Walter rocked his colleague from his slumber.

The men in Walter and Spike's company had been waiting for four days to get on a boat out of France. Hour after hour, day after day, one boat after another came and moored up on the badly damaged harbour walls loading up with servicemen, mostly British, but also French, Polish, Dutch and Belgian.

The boats were all sizes, some were seagoing passenger ships that could take over a thousand men, others Navy warships, whilst others were little more than pleasure boats and yachts, steered by their owners, that could take less than twenty. But every boat that came was joyfully welcomed as their skippers braved the high tides and rough waves of the English Channel in spring time.

"What is it, Wally? Are we getting on a ship yet?" mumbled a weary Spike, who was still half asleep, "I think I can still hear those Panzers you know, they're probably going to blast us out of the water the minute we get on board! That'd just be my luck!"

"Shut up, Spike!" barked Walter.

Much to everyone's surprise, in all the time they had waited to get a place on a boat there hadn't been a single peep out of the German army for the entire time that the evacuation was taking place, and although this unnerved everyone, all the men were so grateful for the truce, if it was, in fact, a truce.

"What did you wake me up for, Wally?" Spike turned over and tried to snuggle back down in his makeshift bed which was more of a nest. He pulled his tin hat back over his eyes but Walter pulled it straight off, "Hey! Watch it, Wally!"

"Look, Spike!" Walter pointed at a ship, a steamer that was pulling in close by.

"It's a *ship*," pronounced Spike, "in case you hadn't noticed, there's quite a lot of 'em about, except none of 'em are collecting us! They're probably gonna leave us here!"

"No, Spike, not the ship the flag," Walter was pointing , "look at the flag!"

"Mmm, funny flag that!" said a disinterested Spike.

"It's not funny at all," said Walter staring angrily at his pal, "it's the flag of the Isle of Man!"

Spike couldn't quite grasp Walter's joy as the ship moored on the harbour wall. He was more interested in going back to sleep.

"What sort of a name is The Rushen Castle anyway?" muttered Spike, "It can't be from the Isle of Man, more likely it's from Moscow or somewhere else in Russia and you never know if you can trust the Ruskies you know!"

"Shut up, Wally! It's a Manx name, Rushen Castle is a Manx name."

"Well it sounds a bit suspect to me!" Grumbled the soldier quietly, "are you sure Uncle Joe's not the captain!"

Apart from soldiers, there were quite a number of bedraggled refugees hanging around the harbour, waiting to see if there were spaces on any boats and if they would be allowed to board them.

Nobody seemed to have a clue as to how the poor civilians managed to get into the sea port because, officially, only soldiers were being allowed to wait to be evacuated. But there were a few wretched souls waiting to board the ships with the soldiers. The men were treating these people with the utmost respect as, on the whole, the soldiers agreed that everyone who was there should be allowed to board the ships and get back to England as long as there were enough spaces for them.

Chapter 30

JACOB'S NEWS

"Becker! Becker!" barked the guard as Jacob sat eating breakfast at a long table with dozens of other men, "Jacob Becker!"

Jacob didn't have any complaints about camp food, it wasn't like the food his mom made at home but it was edible. Generally, the food at the camp was of a decent standard because some of the internees who had been chefs or cooks back home agreed to continue using their skills in the camp. Everyone in the camps worked and got a small weekly wage for their labours, but because food was so important to everyone, the cooks received more than anyone else. Due to rationing and food restrictions there wasn't much variety and there were never pancakes with maple syrup and massive glasses of fresh orange juice for breakfast!

"We used to have pancakes and maple syrup a lot at home," Jacob had mused as they ate their food before his name was called.

"Maple syrup?" asked Terry, licking his lips. Terry Lowe had never actually tried maple syrup so he could only dream what it tasted like but he was sure that it had to be delicious.

"Sure! Always!"

"I'd like to try maple syrup on my pancakes someday," said Terry staring dreamily into his bland bowl of porridge.

"Well, when I get back home I'll send you some, just write down your address for me."

At the camp dining room there was at least something different to eat each day of the week. If it was Tuesday it was bread and jam for breakfast with tea and if it was Sunday it was cornflakes and toast with tea. Today it was porridge with prunes. If the boys hadn't known there was absolutely nothing else to eat neither Jacob nor Terry would have bothered to eat the unappetising looking offering sat in the bottom of their bowls! But what they were served was all they would get so they ate it, all of it!

"Becker!" bellowed the guard for a second time, "Am I talking to myself or what?"

"What?" whispered Jacob. Terry sniggered.

"What was that, Becker?" The guard glared at Jacob.

"I said no, Sir, sorry, Sir," said Jacob getting up.

The guard eyed Jacob suspiciously and then said quietly, "Come with me, lad."

Jacob followed the guard out of the dining room and out of the hotel where everyone in the camp gathered three times a day for their meals, along the deserted promenade and into the building that housed the offices of the camp administrators.

"That office there," pointed the guard with his rifle, the guards always carried rifles. Wolfgang said he thought that most of them weren't loaded, escaping was nearly impossible and they'd heard there was a shortage of ammunition on the island.

"What?" Jacob was confused.

"Go in THERE!" ordered the Guard, "That office! On the table there's a telephone, I'm sure you've heard of the telephone, it's not a new invention! However, it is a British one! Maybe you don't have them in America?"

"Yeah, we do!" Snapped Jacob.

"Well you'll be pleased to know that there's a telephone call for you."

"For me?" Jacob pointed to himself.

"Is there anyone else here or have I mislaid the two dozen other prisoners that I was supposed to bring? Go on lad! Go and answer it!"

"Hello?" said Jacob curiously as he lifted the receiver to his face.

"Jacob," said a voice that Jacob was not expecting to hear, one that he hadn't heard for some time.

"DAD!" Jacob screamed!

"Jacob!"

"Dad! Oh Dad, I never thought I would hear from you again, Dad!"

"I'm so sorry, son. So very, very sorry."

"For what?" asked Jacob.

"For bringing us all back to England, it's all my fault," confessed Carl Becker, "We should have stayed in Concord."

"But you didn't have a choice, Dad."

"Well, maybe I didn't, but you could all have stayed at home, I don't know, but…anyway how are you, Son, are you OK? Are they treating you OK?" Carl, changed the subject abruptly, what was done was done.

"OK, I suppose. I've got a new best friend."

"Yeah?"

"Yeah, he's called Terry Lowe and he's really funny. When I get back home I'm gonna send him some maple syrup!"

"Maple syrup? Great! They tell me you're in the men's camp? What's that like?"

"Oh, not too bad, I'm in a house with a few other men and they're all nice to me, especially Wolfgang, he's really great. Have you heard from Mum, Sarah and Grossmutti?" asked Jacob changing the subject.

"I'm going to speak with them shortly, but I think they're OK, they're on the island too you know, and they're all together in the same house."

"All together?"

"Yes, in a guest house."

"We're in a house but it's just for us prisoners."

"You're not a prisoner, Jacob," Carl said firmly, "just a detainee, and one who shouldn't even be there!"

"It sure seems like a prison, Dad."

Chapter 31

GOOD NEWS AT THE RUSHEN CAMP

It seemed that good news, like lots of other things, was a rare commodity in 1940. Many people in Britain and across Europe didn't seem to have that much to be happy about, but one day, just a few days after her arrival at the Rushen Camp, Elisabeth Becker seemed to have more than her fair share of good news.

Shortly after breakfast, as Elisabeth and Mrs Schwartkopf helped Mrs Simpkins clear up the breakfast dishes, Dr Schmidt came into the dining room waving a note.

"A young lady has just given me zis," she said excitedly, which was very unusual for Dr Schmidt, "it's for you, Elisabeth."

"For me? What is it?"

"It's marked private," added the vet, who was just about to go out for a morning walk with Geli and a couple of older ladies from the house next door. It had quickly become their routine to enjoy morning walks.

Quickly, Elisabeth opened the note and read it.

"Who is it from?" asked Mrs Schwartzkopf curiously. There wasn't ever very much to do in the Rushen Camp so a letter was really exciting.

"It's from Dame Joanna," replied Elisabeth reading the note, "and she wants to see me straight away."

"Well now, Elisabeth, you mustn't keep Dame Joanna waiting," said Mrs Simpkins chuckling, "you just leave these pots, we'll clear up."

"Thank you. I wonder what she wants?"

"Only one way to find out, dear!"

As Elisabeth Becker walked the short distance to Dame Joanna Cruikshank's office, a million and one things were going through her head, most of them bad. Something terrible had happened to Carl? Maybe something had happened to Jacob? They were being told that they would never be able to leave the camp and go home? As she walked the anxiety was quite overwhelming and her heart pounded.

Knock! Knock! She rapped on Dame Joanna's door.

"Come!" called a familiar voice from inside.

Elisabeth opened the door slowly and walked in.

"Ah! Mrs Becker!" said Dame Joanna getting to her feet, she rushed around her desk and pulled a seat forward for Elisabeth, she was grinning broadly. Elisabeth had never seen Dame Joanna even break a smile let alone grin!

"Good news, Mrs Becker!"

Elisabeth let out a sigh of relief, her hand clasped over her mouth as she fought back tears of relief.

"Oh thank goodness!"

"Yes indeed. Two things, firstly…" just as she started to speak, the telephone that was on her desk rang, "…excuse me… Dame Joanna Cruikshank!" she said into the black receiver, "Yes, yes…very good, ah yes…good morning, Miss Daniels,…of course, of course, I've been expecting it, put him through, Miss Daniels, and I'll put her on the line."

Dame Joanna passed the telephone receiver to Elisabeth, "Call for you, Mrs Becker."

Elisabeth warily took the phone her thoughts racing, "For me?" *Who could want to speak to me?*

"Hello?" she said slowly.

"Elisabeth?" spoke a familiar voice.

"CARL!" she screamed, "OH CARL!"

"Elisabeth, it's great to hear your voice, my darling!" Carl held the telephone away from his ear!

"Oh Carl, Carl! I've been so worried, so terribly worried! How are you?" Elisabeth's eyes were filling with tears.

"Here you go," whispered Dame Joanna passing a handkerchief.

"Thank you," mouthed Elisabeth.

"I'm fine, busy you know, working real hard, I can't say too much you understand."

"Yes, yes, I understand."

"But you? How are you? Are they treating you alright? You hear such terrible things about what goes on over there!"

"No, no I'm fine, really fine. It's not too bad at all here.

We're treated very well, our landlady, Mrs Simpkins is really lovely, she's made us feel so welcome and Port Erin and Port St Mary are such beautiful places."

"I'm glad to hear it. And Sarah, how is she? Getting more and more beautiful I expect?"

"She's great, growing up so fast. She's got a new friend, Laila, and she spends almost all day every day at the beach."

"At the beach? Can't be bad!" joked Carl, "and Mutti, how is Mutti?"

"She's very well too, she found the journey a long one and was very tired for a couple of days but she's being taken care of by her very own doctor."

"Her own doctor? Really? How come?"

"Yes, her name's Dr Schmidt, we met her on the trip over, she's really lovely and Mutti is enjoying being looked after, they've become really good friends."

"I hear Jacob's OK, I've just spoken to him, and he's well," said Carl.

"Oh, thank God, Carl! I'd not heard anything." Elisabeth choked slightly trying not to break down in floods of tears.

Dame Joanna coughed and passed a note, which read 'I have good news about your son.'

"Anyway my love," said Carl, "I have to go, believe me I'm hoping to come and see you real soon."

"I can't wait. I love you, Carl."

"I love you too, Honey, and I hope we can all go home real soon."

"That makes two of us."

"Anyway I better go, I love you, Elisabeth."

"I love you too!"

The phone went dead and Elisabeth sat staring ahead in stunned silence until Dame Joanna coughed again.

"Oh, sorry," said Elisabeth.

"I have news about Jacob."

Chapter 32

THE TWO STRANGERS BOARD
THE RUSHEN CASTLE

"Look," whispered Johan into Gertrude's ear, in the current climate being heard speaking German could be dangerous, "you see that ship over there," he nodded to the ship that had just moored, "The Rushen Castle."

"Yes," replied Gertrude who was very much a shadow of her former glamorous self. She'd lost almost a quarter of her body weight and the lustrous quality of her pampered complexion had given way to blotchy skin. Her once sparkling eyes that gave away her sense of fun were now slightly sunken and dark rimmed and told of the anguish she faced daily.

"Well, I've just had a word with the ship's mate and there are a couple of places on board for us."

"Have you paid him enough?" In the chaos of war only hard currency like gold could be relied upon to buy favours.

"Yes, yes I think so."

Johan and Gertrude were now using Dutch passports and, in public, speaking Dutch to each other, although Johan spoke fluent and Gertrude passable English, it was this ability to speak a variety of languages that was allowing them to find their way through the confusion that was the British withdrawal from France.

For the best part of a year the pair had wandered across the wilderness that was the war zone of western Europe, escaping the Nazis' grip which was slowly tightening on the world they once knew. But Johan and Gertrude were determined to get across to England any way they could.

By a stroke of good luck, just over a month ago, the pair had managed to attach themselves to some members of the British Expeditonary Force and crossed into the rapidly reducing British occupied zone in northern France and since then they had been following the painfully slow withdrawal northwards.

The months on the road, always on the run, endlessly looking over their shoulders had taken their toll, more so on Gertrude than Johan. Now her hair was cut short and was rarely washed, and she couldn't even remember the last time she had a bath.

"Come on! Come on!" said Johan, "our ship's leaving soon."

Quickly, Gertrude followed Johan on board The Rushen Castle, she couldn't quite believe she was boarding a ship at last, and very shortly she would be leaving for England. Soon she would go to London and find her daughter, Laila. But her feelings of excitement at seeing her daughter, thoughts that had kept her going over the long, dangerous months, were tinged with total desperation about her husband. *Where was Ahren? Was he still in Berlin? What had happened to him? Was he even still alive?*

"Here, Miss," said a young soldier, holding out his hand to help Gertrude Levy onto the ship, "let me help you."

Almost to a man the British soldiers had been polite, friendly and helpful.

"Thank you," said Gertrude summoning up a weak smile.

"My name's Walter Simpkins," said the man.

"Thank you, Walter, my name's Gertrude, Gertrude Lehare."

"Nice to meet you, Gertrude, where are you going?"

"To my family in London, and you?"

"Home to the Isle of Man, with a bit of luck."

"The Isle of Man? I don't think I know of that island."

"Oh, it's the best place in the world, Gertrude, a little island between England and Ireland, it's a paradise and I live on the very southern tip of it in a place called Port Erin. It's paradise!"

Chapter 33

SHOCKING HEADLINES
DISCUSSED IN PARLIAMENT

"Can the honourable member assure the House that these headlines are in fact a pack of lies?" asked a furious backbench member of the House of Commons.

"Err...," Home Secretary, Sir John Anderson, hadn't read his copy of the Daily Mail that morning over breakfast, preferring The Times to accompany his boiled egg and buttered toast soldiers.

Hurriedly, the Home Secretary was passed a copy of that morning's paper and he hastily scanned the headline.

"For the benefit of those members who haven't read the Daily Mail," the backbencher sneered at the Home Secretary, "the headline declares that some of the people interned on the Isle of Man under Regulation 18B are in fact having a whale of a time!"

The crowded chamber roared in anger!

"I must protest..." Sir John tried to interrupt, but was having trouble being heard over the din.

"That while people...working people, over here on the mainland are struggling with the pressures of war with Hitler... the pressures of rationing...the pressure of imminent invasion... the bombings."

"Mr Speaker, I really MUST protest..."

"WHILE we are at war our enemies, yes, ENEMIES," screamed the MP, "are having a holiday at our expense!"

As the speaker struggled to contain the uproar, Sir John slumped back in his seat, took a long sip of whisky and looked down at the headline.

"HOLIDAY CAMPS! German women prisoners on Isle of Man swim NAKED in sea each day as Britain faces war with Germany."

Chapter 34

MR BOBBINS PAYS UP

Life couldn't have been more different in the south-western part of the Isle of Man than in London. The first few days and weeks at the Rushen Camp did, indeed, feel more like a summer holiday at the seaside than imprisonment in an internment camp. Whilst many of the women were desperate to get off the island and get home to their families, for some it was an adventure of a lifetime.

For ten year old Sarah Becker and her young friend Laila Levy, the gloriously endless days were spent on the beautiful beaches, swimming in the sea and exploring the coves and rocks. The girls were enjoying themselves so much there was barely any time to think of the worries of their past life. The girls were young enough to enjoy their lives and live for the moment. There weren't that many other girls of their age so they enjoyed each other's company each and every day and discovered that they were building a firm friendship.

Since the arrival of the women and girls in Port Erin and Port St Mary, the Manx weather had been hot and sunny every single day and this had led to most of the women enjoying the seaside just like Sarah and Laila.

The routine was the same each morning as an endless stream of well to do German women could be seen making their way to the beach with their baskets and towels. Some even got a reputation for not bothering to wear bathing costumes when they went in the sea which was acceptable in most areas of Europe but a habit unheard of in Britain. This caused quite a stir amongst the locals and even caught the attention of reporters from far away London!

As Laila and Sarah bounced happily into the house after an enjoyable morning of swimming and exploring they were just in time to sit down for lunch. As they pulled their chairs up to the table they noticed that Elisabeth had a huge grin across her face.

This was really unusual as Elisabeth was, up to now, constantly worrying about the whereabouts of her husband and especially her son. Virtually nothing could take her mind off poor Jacob. She was worried sick about what had happened to him.

Only once in the past week had Elisabeth thought about something else and that was something that Sarah and Laila preferred to actually forget about, the purchase of bathing costumes!

Laila and Sarah had been so keen to buy swimming costumes that first day so that they could rush off to the beach that they had paid for two costumes worth one and sixpence with a pound note and not bothered whether they were given coins, bus tokens or even buttons as change!

A pound note in 1940 was a lot of money, especially when the average wage of a skilled workman was in the region of one pound five shillings per week. Something was not quite right with the purchase!

"Where's the rest of change for the swimsuits, Honey?" asked Elisabeth after the girls had returned from the beach on that first afternoon.

"The *rest* of the change?" asked a bewildered Sarah, looking at her friend and shrugging her shoulders.

"Rest of the change?" whispered Laila shaking her head.

"Yeah, the *rest* of the change, Sarah, Laila, it's what you get when you buy something that's not worth a lot, like bathing costumes and you pay with something as big as a pound note!"

148

"Oh!" Replied Sarah sheepishly.

"Oh, what?" Elisabeth was getting annoyed.

"Oh, the man didn't give me much change."

"Not much change? But I gave you a pound note! There should have been a lot of change!"

"I just gave the money to the man in the shop," confessed Sarah in total honesty.

"Well, how much did the costumes actually cost, Sarah?" Elisabeth frowned.

"I don't remember," this wasn't a lie, Sarah had been so excited to actually have a costume and be able to go swimming that she couldn't remember how much they had cost, or how much change she'd been given, anyway she didn't understand English money, American money was so much easier, with their hundred cents in a dollar, she couldn't be bothered with the silly English coins and notes.

"Do you remember, Laila?" asked Elisabeth, turning her attention on Sarah's young friend.

Laila thought for a minute then shook her head, "No, Mrs Becker, I really don't, sorry."

Just at that moment Mrs Simpkins came in to serve tea.

"Is there a problem, dear?" she asked, sensing the atmosphere.

"Oh, just that I gave the girls a pound note to buy their two swimming costumes and they only gave me a couple of shillings change."

"Is that all? Well, those costumes won't have cost more than one shilling and sixpence at the most, there should have been plenty of change, certainly more than a couple of bob!"

"That's what I thought," agreed Elisabeth glaring at her daughter.

"No don't blame them, Elisabeth," said Mrs Simpkins,"He's got a bit of a reputation for this kind of thing has Mr Bobbins!"

"What do you mean?"

"Oh, he's a skinflint, a right royal one! As tight as..." Mrs Simpkins paused, "...well, let's just say that he's well known for it, I'm sure he saw these two innocent young girls coming. He will have known that they don't understand English money, he's making a fortune out of all this business! I bet he didn't even put the note in the till! I bet it went straight under the counter!"

"Well! Did he put it in the till?" asked Elisabeth, staring at the girls.

"I can't remember," sighed Sarah.

"I can," said Laila, "he didn't, he didn't put it in the till, he put it in his jacket pocket."

"Right!" said Mrs Simpkins with a determined look on her face, "Come with me!"

All three, Elisabeth, Laila and Sarah got up and followed Mrs Simpkins out of the house. Up the road they marched behind her. Even though she was an older, larger lady she could certainly walk quickly when she wanted to and anyone who was in her path quickly got out of the way. The girls and Elisabeth had to trot just to keep up with her.

BANG! BANG! BANG! Mrs Simpkins rapped on the door of the shop, which was closed as it was almost six o'clock. She hit the door so hard that it could have come off its hinges given a few more thumps!

BANG! BANG! BANG! She was determined and wouldn't take no for an answer.

"Maybe he's gone home," said Elisabeth, "there's no one about," she peered through the windows, "the shop's in total darkness."

"Nonsense! He lives above the shop," replied Mrs Simpkins firmly, "he hasn't gone anywhere!"

BANG! BANG! BANG!

"Go away! We're closed!" somebody called in a muffled voice from upstairs.

Mrs Simpkins backed away from the door and peered up.

"I will not go away! And I know you're closed, James Bobbins!" she bellowed angrily, "I want a word with you!"

"Won't it wait until tomorrow, Mrs Simpkins? My tea's on the table!" protested the shop owner, not daring to show his face.

"No it won't, Mr Bobbins!"

"Oh dear!" muttered Bobbins .

Mrs Simpkins moved back to the door and after a couple of minutes the lights started going on in the shop, then the bolts on the door were being slid across.

The door opened a tiny crack and just an eye appeared staring out.

"Yes?" Mr Bobbins said in a feeble voice.

"I'll give you 'yes'," said Mrs Simpkins, mimicking Bobbins.

"Is there something the matter, Mrs Simpkins?" The eye stared out at the girls. He immediately knew why they were there. The eye at the door started blinking uncontrollably.

"Well, maybe you can work it out, Bobbins! I see your eye recognises these two girls!"

"I don't know what you're talking about, Mrs Simpkins!

I've never seen these two before in my entire life!"

"Oh, I think you have! You're blinking too much, that's a sign that you're lying! It's a well known fact! Admit you've seen them before, Bobbins! Admit it now!"

"No, I don't think so," lied Bobbins but his eye blinked the truth.

"Well, I do! There's far too much blinking going on for my liking, man!"

Elisabeth, Sarah and Laila stared at each other, they'd never realised a blink could give away so much, they all thought they would have to be more careful in future!

"I swear I don't!" The eye was looking extraordinarily strained and bloodshot now and almost paralysed with so much nonstop blinking!

"Well, maybe I should go straight to PC Whiting and explain it to him?"

"No, no!" said the voice that was still behind the closed door, now the eye was staring, panic stricken, "I don't think we need to involve PC Whiting! Hahaha!" A pathetic little laugh came from behind the door.

"Stop laughing, man!" bellowed Mrs Simpkins.

"Sorry."

"I think you owe these girls some more change from their pound note!"

"Pound note?" protested Bobbins who wasn't going to give up easily. The blinking started again.

"Right!" Mrs Simpkins turned and walked away, "I'm going to see PC Whiting!"

"No!" shouted Bobbins, at last his entire chubby face appeared in half shadow, "Wait there!"

The door slammed shut, and after a long pause opened again, this time wide enough for a hand to push through. There was money in the hand and before the cash could drop to the ground, Mrs Simpkins showed lightning fast reactions and caught it all.

"Take your stupid money!" cursed Mr Bobbins from behind the door, "I don't want it anyway!"

"Shall I tell everyone in the camp that?" asked Elisabeth.

"No! No!" answered Bobbins quickly, "I didn't actually mean that I wouldn't serve…"

"Good evening to you, Mr Bobbins!" snapped Mrs Simpkins furiously, turning on her heels and heading home. As Elisabeth and the girls scurried after their landlady, Sarah glanced over her shoulder at the shop, the hand was still there waving pathetically and the eye could be seen blinking away in the shadows.

"Look, Laila!" she whispered to her friend, "He's still blinking!"

"Blinking 'eck!" snorted Laila, laughing.

"Bye Mr Bobbins' eye!!" shouted Sarah laughing.

Chapter 35

NEWS OF A MOVE FOR JACOB AND TERRY

In the permanently confused state of the internment camps on the Isle of Man, the warm summer days became weeks and weeks became months. May passed into June and before they knew it, the boring, routine filled days had entered the month of July.

The chaos led to massive administration delays that were inevitable and with thousands and thousands of internees arriving each week, very quickly the camps all across the island became full to bursting point.

It became quite clear to the clerks and civil servants in far away London that solutions to the serious problems of overcrowding in the camps had to be found, and quickly!

When she discovered that young Jacob Becker had been wrongly billeted in the men's camp in Douglas, Dame Joanna Cruikshank immediately put in a request that he should be allowed to join his mother, grandmother and sister at her camp, the Rushen Camp in the far south west of the island. Jacob was a twelve year old boy after all and that meant he should not be in the men's camp.

But somehow Dame Joanna's letter must have ended up on a skyscraper high pile of paperwork in the office at the men's camp in Douglas, ignored and gathering dust.

"Oy! Let's be 'aving you, Becker!" yelled a camp guard as he burst into Jacob's bedroom early one morning. It must have barely been six o'clock because the house was totally silent.

"Wh…wh…what?" mumbled a sleepy Jacob who, for a moment, wasn't even sure where he was. He rubbed his eyes as he sat up in his bed.

"You're going home, lad!" replied the Guard, grinning.

"Home?"

"Are you deaf or is it just because you're a Yank?"

"To America?" said Jacob, ignoring the jibe.

"Err…" the guard thought for a moment. "Err…to Canada I think, but that's near enough isn't it? Now come on lad, there's a few spare places and the governor thought about you, you being a Yank an all! He thought you might like to go home!"

"Oh," said Jacob rubbing his eyes, "are my family going too?"

"How should I know, lad? I just know what I've been told, no more, no less, now come on! Let's be 'aving you!"

"Can I come?" asked Terry in his best American accent that he'd learned by copying Jacob. The accent was not terribly good though.

"Are you a Yank too? I didn't know there were two of you?"

"Naw, I'm no Yank, Sir, I'm Canadian," said Terry, quite convincingly.

The guard eyed Terry suspiciously and scratched his head. He thought long and hard, well at least long!

"Are you really Canadian?" he asked squinting.

"Sure!"

"Well, get a move on too! Five minutes and I want to see you two out the front! You're leaving in ten!"

As the guard disappeared Jacob turned to Terry.

"Boy, that was the worst Canadian accent I've ever heard, Terry!"

"Well you taught me!"

"I did not teach you an accent like that, no Americans speak like that."

"But I'm not American, Jakey Boy, I'm Canadian! It fooled him though didn't it!"

"Anyone could fool an old codger like him, but why do you want to come to Canada?"

"Why not? It's got to be better than sitting around here all day! And if I don't like it I can always come home!"

Chapter 36

THE NAZIS IN THE WOMEN'S
CAMP CAUSE TROUBLE

Elisabeth Becker and her family had very little to do with any
of the Nazi women that were at the Rushen Camp but she had
heard stories about how nasty they were with the Jewish women
and their families. They called them terrible names and spat at
them as they walked past.

At first the Nazi women had kept themselves to themselves
but things changed after the camp authorities had asked them to
sign forms to say they didn't support Hitler's government. This
made them angry.

Not only did the women refuse to condemn Hitler, they said
it was their right under an international agreement called the
Geneva Convention to swear oaths of allegiance to their own
Government.

After some of the Nazi women complained, Dame Joanna
said she had no choice but follow this up with the Swiss
Embassy in London. As there was no German Embassy,
Switzerland was looking after the interests of German people
in the UK, and the Swiss Embassy came back with a very
strange proposal.

The Swiss said that all Germans living in Britain did have
a right to swear oaths of allegiance to Hitler's Government and
that if they did so they would get monthly payments from Berlin
which the Swiss Embassy would then send to the camps on the
Isle of Man. They also said that under the Geneva Convention,

the internees had the right to be repatriated or sent home straight away.

"So," said Frau Henkel, one of the leaders of the Nazi women, in excellent English to Dame Joanna, "the Swiss Embassy has given you an answer I see, no?" She was rudely peering over the desk at the letter in front of Dame Joanna and trying to read it upside down.

"Yes, indeed," replied Dame Joanna, looking down at the long legal document, "they certainly have."

"And what do they say?" Henkel wanted to reach out and snatch the letter but didn't dare.

"They say, Frau Henkel, that all German citizens have the right to swear an oath of allegiance to the German Government..."

"Ah yes...and?"

"And that Berlin will send a monthly allowance to every person who does so..."

"Very generous of our Government don't you think, no? And?"

"And?"

"Yes, 'and'!" her voice rose sharply as she spoke, her anger barely contained, "do they say that we should be sent back home to the Fatherland immediately, Madam Commandant?"

"Ah, Frau Henkel, unfortunately the bottom part of the letter has been blacked out, for security reasons you understand, so I am unable to tell you what else it says," Dame Joanna looked Frau Henkel straight in the eye.

"Under the Geneva Convention we must be repatriated at once!" shouted Henkel, rising from her chair, "I know my rights!"

Yet Dame Joanna was quick to respond and didn't take kindly to being shouted at!

"Let me remind you! Under international law your Government should not have invaded Poland, Madam!" replied Dame Joanna calmly as Henkel stormed from the office.

After word spread about the response from the Swiss Embassy many German women at the camp signed the oath of allegiance to Berlin and then availed themselves of the monthly allowance which they eagerly spent in the shops in the village, but such were the feelings of anger that they should be sent home, relations between the camp authorities and the women became very strained. Strikes and sit-ins were organised and the women refused to do any chores or work around the villages.

This was also the start of the terrible bullying of Jewish women. Most of the Jews were sensible enough to avoid contact with the Nazis as much as possible. But it only really came to Elisabeth Becker and her family's attention one evening after the night time curfew had been called.

"Mom, we can hear someone outside!" said Sarah as she and Laila appeared in the lounge at nine thirty, which was well after their bedtime.

"Can you, dear?" asked Mr Simpkins, who was sipping his hot milk, reading the newspaper and listening to the radio.

"Are you sure you didn't dream it?" asked Geli, who had got quite used to peaceful island life and enjoyed her evenings with Mr and Mrs Simpkins.

"No I didn't, Grossmutti!" answered Sarah crossly, "because I wasn't asleep and because Laila heard it too!" Sarah turned to her friend who nodded her support.

"Yes, Mrs Becker, I heard it too."

"Should you go outside and take a look, Father?" Mrs Simpkins always called Mr Simpkins father through force of habit even though all of their children were grown up and had left home.

"Oh alright," he said putting his mug down and getting to his feet, "I'll have a look."

Less than a minute later Mr Simpkins burst through the door dragging something along with him. For a minute nobody could quite make out what he was struggling to pull through the door, it could have been a heavy sack of potatoes or corn for all they could make out, then it dawned on the ladies.

Laila and Sarah screamed in horror.

"Oh my goodness!" said Mrs Simpkins, rushing to help her husband.

"Oh dear, oh dear!" gasped Geli, through her hands.

"Here, put her on the sofa!" said Elisabeth, rushing to help, "and Sarah," she said turning to her daughter who was stood shaking by the door, "you'll be OK, honey, now can you please go and get Dr Schmidt from her room, be real quick!"

"I'll go too!" said Laila grabbing Sarah's hand as the girls set off up the stairs in a state of shock.

Dr Schmidt, although a vet, was the best human doctor anyone could ever want because she was so gentle and careful. She examined the poor woman that Mr Simpkins had discovered outside his house and cleaned up her cuts and bruises with some iodine and warm water that Mrs Simpkins had brought from the kitchen.

"I'm afraid I don't have any medicine," said Dr Schmidt.

"We'll take her to the hospital when she's fit to move," said Mr Simpkins.

"What do you think happened to her?" asked Sarah to her mum.

"I don't know, honey," replied Elisabeth, "I really don't," but, although she said this to her young daughter, she had a good idea who could have been behind the vicious attack because the lady had a big 'J' written in spidery writing on the back of her hand.

"Well, I think she's only cut and bruised," said Dr Schmidt, "there are no broken bones and I hope she might wake up soon. But we must be very careful with her, she may be very confused."

"It's good for this poor soul that you're here, Dr Schmidt," said her friend, Geli.

Just as they were speaking the lady started to come around, she started muttering under her breath in German and Dr Schmidt had to move very close to her mouth to hear her, after a while she spoke to her quietly.

"Please don't be alarmed," she whispered, "you are safe now and I am a doctor, you're not badly hurt."

"Where am I?" asked the woman, barely able to open her eyes, which were badly bruised.

"They're going to be whoppers! Real black eyes!" said Mr Simpkins, "I know a black eye when I see one."

"Make yourself useful, Father," snapped his wife, "bring the lady a hot drink will you and a blanket!"

"You're safe and sound at Mrs Simpkins house," said Elisabeth in German.

"Am I in England?" asked the woman, who was still having trouble focussing on the people who crowded around her, "I thought I was in England."

"Well, sort of," replied Elisabeth, "but not quite, you're on the Isle of Man."

"In Port Erin!" added Laila.

"Oh," said Elisabeth turning around to the girls, "I'd forgotten you were there, why don't you leave this poor lady in peace, go on, go back to your beds, it's getting quite late. I'll come up and see you in a minute"

As Elisabeth whispered to the girls the poor woman suddenly sat bolt upright! The abrupt movement shocked everyone and they all jumped clear of her in case something horrible was happening to her.

"Laila!" shouted the woman in a strong, clear voice.

"Yes," said Laila quietly, and feeling a little scared, she slowly crept to safety behind Geli, who stroked her hair gently.

"Laila!" the woman shouted again, now her arms were outstretched, calling the girl to her.

"Yes, I'm Laila."

"Laila, don't you recognise me, my darling?" said the woman.

"Sorry," said Laila politely, "I don't think I know you."

"It's me," said the woman sobbing, "it's me, Mutti!"

"Mutti?" said Laila, staring in disbelief at the wretched woman, "My Mutti?" Her eyes were filling with tears as she choked back the sob in her voice. Everyone in the room stared.

"Yes, yes my love it's me! Your Mutti, Gertrude Levy!"

Chapter 37

THE ARANDORA STAR

It was still very early morning as Jacob and Terry got to the docks at Douglas and as they did, they noticed that the entire skyline seemed to be filled with an enormous white ship. Their eyes simultaneously stared from the ship at the dockside following its mountainous bulk as it rose up towards the sky. It was higher than any building that Terry had ever seen and had two smoke stackers bellowing out black plumes of soot into the clear morning sky.

"Wowee! It's the Titanic!" said Terry, nudging Jacob's arm and grinning like a Cheshire cat.

"What?" said Jacob, staring at his friend, he couldn't quite believe what he'd just said, but then again this was Terry Lowe! Terry Lowe came out with the most unbelievable things!

"The Titanic," nodded Terry towards the immense bulk of the ship, "that's it, Jakey boy!"

"The Titanic?" scoffed Jacob.

"Yeah."

"But how can it be the Titanic, Terry? The Titanic is lying at the bottom of the Atlantic Ocean! It's miles and miles down!"

"What?" This was shocking news to Terry and clearly knocked him sideways. He stopped stock still and stared at his young friend.

"It sank in 1912," continued Jacob.

"Did it? It sank? Are you sure?"

"Yeah, sank. It was hit by an enormous iceberg and then it sank to the bottom of the ocean. Hundreds and hundreds of people died," Jacob had studied all about the Titanic at school.

"Well, of course I knew it was hit by an iceberg, everyone knows that! But I didn't know that it had sunk!" said Terry with a really disappointed look on his face.

"Er, Terry!" explained Jacob, "the iceberg bashed a massive hole in the ship's side, how do you think it was supposed to continue sailing with water flooding into it?"

"Dunno," he shrugged.

"It's the Arandora Star, lads," said one of the men at the docks, "and you're really lucky that it's stopped for you, it's almost full, they're taking you as a favour to the chief."

"Oh," said Jacob.

"But I thought they were only taking Americans," the man nodded at Terry.

"Actually, I'm Canadian," said Terry adopting his bad accent once again, "she's taking me home, my friend."

As they walked up the steep ramp and onto the ship, the man seemed keen to tell them all about the boat in question.

"Been the pride of the Blue Star Line for over thirteen years now, she has," he said, "a first class ship she is too, more used to taking high class people across the Atlantic than taking a load of Germans to Canada."

The man didn't seem too bothered about what Jacob and Terry thought, he was just eager to tell the boys everything that he knew, which was a lot!

"Aye," he continued, "she's over 512 feet long and her beam is over 68 feet, impressive eh?"

"Very," agreed Jacob, staring at his friend.

"And do you know her tonnage?" asked the man.

"No," said Terry, yawning, "I bet you do though!"

"I do! 14,694 tons, not bad, eh?"

"Not bad," agreed Jacob, who hoped that if he answered the man he might leave them alone more quickly.

"Well, this is where I leave you two, I really wish I could come with you."

"We bloomin' don't," whispered Terry to Jacob as the man walked away.

"Oy, you two!" called a guard, "Hurry up, we're sailing in five minutes, get yourself over here, quick smart!"

Within minutes of Jacob and Terry boarding, the impressive liner, that had originally been known as just the Arandora, weighed anchor and powered up her engines, filling the sky with black smoke, ready for her long voyage across the Atlantic ocean bound for St John's, Newfoundland and then on to Canada.

Chapter 38

FULL TO BURSTING!
THE SIMPKINS HOUSE

The Simpkins' house was already full to bursting when Gertrude Levy had arrived but young Laila, along with Elisabeth and Mrs Simpkins felt they had to see the Camp Commandant straight away. They had begged Dame Joanna to allow Gertrude to stay with them at Mrs Simpkins house because of their fears that she would be attacked again at the camp.

"Please, Dame Joanna, please!" begged Laila, "She's so badly hurt."

"Yes, I am fully aware of the extent of her injuries, Laila," replied Dame Joanna gently, "but Mrs Simpkins house is already full and I don't want to move anyone out."

"Oh, Dame Joanna, what if it happens again, what if those people attack her again!" sobbed Laila.

"Next time they might not just beat her up, Dame Joanna, next time they might kill her!" added Elisabeth.

Dame Joanna Cruikshank sat and thought things through long and hard, she took some papers out of a drawer and looked at some plans. She shuffled the papers and tapped her pencil against her desk all the while muttering under her breath.

"And what do you think, Mrs Simpkins?" she asked the kindly landlady.

"Well, I'm not saying it won't be a squeeze, Dame Joanna," said Mrs Simpkins, looking over at Laila, "but we've always managed somehow so I'm sure we'll cope! And I can see how worried Laila here is about her mother who has, after all, had quite an experience."

"Quite so," responded Dame Joanna, who sighed, "very well, Laila, if Mrs Simpkins is sure she can manage, then your mother can stay with you at her house."

Chapter 39

THE BOMBING INTENSIFIES

As the summer had worn on, the bombing raids on the United Kingdom by the Luftwaffe had grown gradually fiercer. The south east of England was worst hit but ports around the entire United Kingdom, like Sunderland, Glasgow and Liverpool were also heavily bombed.

As the bombardment progressed it became very obvious that the RAF was outnumbered by their German counterparts and even though the British factories were working twenty four hours a day building more and more Spitfires and Hurricanes, the factories in Germany were building more and more of their Messchersmidt 109s.

But again and again the radar network that was the pride and joy of the British government saved the day by giving the RAF pilots a minimum of twenty minutes head start on the Germans. This enabled them to scramble and be in the air ready to do battle with the approaching Messerschmidt 109s as they headed towards the British Isles . But one day at the start of July this all changed.

It was still early morning at Bawdsey Manor when the telephone in Carl Becker's bedroom rang startling him.

"Err...hello," he said sleepily as he struggled to focus.

"Carl, get yourself down to my office quickly, will you!" It was Professor Wilson.

"Jim? What is it? What's the matter?"

"Just get down here, we've got a problem with the network. They've hit it. It's down."

Within three minutes Carl had hastily dressed, pulled on his socks and shoes and was barging into Professor Wilson's office and running his fingers anxiously through his blonde hair.

"They can't have! What is it, Jim? What's happened?"

"It's true, the network has been broken."

"What? How?" Asked Carl.

"Last night German planes targeted a specific part of the network, taking out six towers. They knew exactly what they were doing. Knew what they were aiming for."

"Six towers?"

"Yes, six."

"But six is enough to…"

"To break the circuit?" Jim finished the sentence.

"Yes!"

"Well it did, it broke it, the system has been broken and now the network isn't working. As I said, they knew exactly what they were doing," Professor Jim Wilson looked like he'd been up most of the night.

"So, are you telling me that we don't have any radar at all now?" Asked the American.

"No, I'm not saying that. We do have some radar coverage, some, but there are big holes in it."

"How big?" Mumbled Carl who had sat down with his head in his hands.

"Big enough to get dozens of their heavy bombers through with no one here to see and stop them!"

Carl rubbed his forehead and sighed, "This is what I'd feared all along, Jim."

"Me too, Carl, believe me! Me too!"

There was silence for a couple of minutes as both men considered all the problems and possibilities in their own heads. Each man was searching for answers or solutions. For a short while it was as if time had stood still in Professor Wilson's office. It was Carl who spoke first.

"I think my improvements are ready to go live, Jim," he muttered cautiously.

"Are you sure, Carl?"

"No...not sure, but it'll take days and days, maybe weeks to repair the towers, while my system could be up and running by this evening."

"Are you sure you want to try it now?" asked Wilson.

"Yes, I'm sure," Carl said firmly, "let's hope that the first of July will be a day that goes down in history as the day the Germans couldn't break our radar network under any circumstances!"

Chapter 40

THE FEELING ON THE MAINLAND

The fact that the Arandora Star, along with two other ships, were carrying internees to Canada and another one, the Duneda, which was destined for Australia, was a result of a series of reports over the past few months in a number of British newspapers.

Officially, the British Government in distant Whitehall, London, had decided that the number of internees on the Isle of Man was becoming critical, the island was becoming swamped and soon would be overflowing with aliens, so something drastic needed to be done to address the situation.

But unofficially the Government, like many other British Governments before, were responding with a knee jerk reaction to damning reports in the British press that many of the prisoners on the Isle of Man were living in conditions closely akin to holiday camps rather than prison camps.

How was this fair and reasonable, declared the press, when many people on the mainland struggled each and every day to make ends meet, especially since rationing of food had been brought in?

More than one article featured stories about the Rushen Camp, with its rich German ladies who spent every morning shopping for high priced clothes and every afternoon sunbathing on the white sandy beaches of the island and swimming in the sea. The articles said that these women were living in luxurious hotels and guest houses that many Brits back home could only dream about.

After the Daily Mail exclusive, more and more papers ran reports of the hedonistic lifestyles of the internees and especially about those who didn't even bother to wear bathing suits on the beach!

"We've got to do something about these rumours!" said the Home Secretary, Sir John Anderson, to his assistant, James Smethers, as he folded up yet another newspaper and placed it on his desk.

"I don't quite know what we *can* do, Sir," replied Smethers.

"I'm sick and tired of seeing reports like this, man, can't you see that I'm becoming a laughing stock!"

"Oh, I'm sure you're not, Sir."

"Are these stories true, Smethers?" asked the Home Secretary, pointing to the paper, "I mean, is this how they're spending their days? Shopping, sunbathing and swimming?"

"I have had reports that overcrowding is becoming a major problem on the island," replied Smethers reading from a list of reports and not entirely addressing the question, "I can confirm that conditions, on the whole, on the island are very basic, and internees are, in effect, treated like prisoners of war."

"On the whole?" The Home Secretary had developed a reputation for his attention to detail, "What do you mean? On the whole?"

"The reports of the shopping, swimming and sun bathing, Sir...," continued Smethers reluctantly. "...the reports that some of the ladies in the..."

"The Rushen Camp, Smethers...The Rushen Camp! And these reports that some of the ladies swim and sunbathe all day without any bathing costumes? Is it true?"

"Err..."

"Err? Err what?"

"Err...well, yes Sir. It is true."

"Well this won't do, Smethers," snapped the Home Secretary, "it just won't do at all! We need to do something about the situation, or at least we need to be seen to be doing something about the situation. Do you understand what I'm saying?"

"Loud and clear, Sir…what about the possibility of sharing some of the load or burden, Sir?"

"What do you mean?" The Home Secretary stared over the top of his spectacles.

"Well, do you remember during the Great War, there were many thousands of people, German people, interned by our government?"

"Yes, of course, everyone remembers!"

"Well, although many thousands of them were interned here and on the Isle of Man…"

"At the... em…that's right, the Knockaloe camp," added the Home Secretary remembering.

"The very same, Sir. Well, although there were many internees in the British Isles shall we say, there were many, many thousands more interned overseas in the colonies."

"The colonies? Are you telling me that there were internment camps around the commonwealth, Smethers?"

"Very much so, Sir, thousands were interned around the commonwealth."

"So what exactly are you proposing, man?"

"I propose that we share or at least, be seen to share, the burden of alien internment with say, Canada and Australia, they're both huge countries and both have plenty of space, perhaps this would be a good move in the first instance."

"How many ships do you propose?"

"Three, maybe four to begin with, I think."

Chapter 41

THE SINKING OF THE ARANDORA STAR

Because of the decision of the Home Secretary in London to share the burden of the alien internment, Jacob Becker and Terry Lowe along with over five hundred other men were starting the long and dangerous journey in the unarmed and unprotected former cruise ship, the Arandora Star, across the U-boat infested seas of the North Atlantic to internment camps in Canada.

"Jake! Hey, Jake!" puffed Terry Lowe, running along the deck bumping into anyone who was unfortunate enough to get in his way.

"Over here, Terry! I'm over here!" called out Jacob.

Terry had just rushed up from the lower decks with important news.

"Jake! Huh..., huh...," he panted.

"Deep breaths, Terry!" warned Jacob calmly, demonstrating how to breathe.

"OK," said Terry, following Jacob's actions and orders, "OK, I'm breathing OK now!"

"Right, what's the matter?" Asked Jacob.

"Jake, I'm not so sure it was such a good idea to come on this trip anymore," Terry shook his head and scowled. They were less than two days into their long journey.

Throughout the crowded decks of the Arandora Star the ship was rife with rumours about the dangers of sailing across the Atlantic Ocean with the Wermacht's most lethal and almost completely invisible weapon lurking under the grey waters waiting to blow up any passing ship.

"What?" Jacob was on deck enjoying the fresh air, daydreaming about being at home and watching the north coast of Ireland disappear gradually into the distance.

"Jake! They're all saying that this part of the ocean is really dangerous you know," gasped Terry still panting hard.

"Breathe, Terry!" warned Jacob, "In…out. In…out!"

"OK, in…" Terry sucked in some air, held his breath and blew it out, "..out! In...out!"

"In what way dangerous?" asked Jacob.

"Lots of U-boats lurking about!"

"Oh U-boats, yeah, I suppose...," said Jacob starting to scan the seas all around the ship suspiciously, he knew that submarines or U-boats as they were called had been a lethal weapon for the Germans over the past year or so. His dad had told him all about them.

As an island, during the war Britain was reliant especially for food and other supplies from its overseas allies and the Germans knew that to make life really difficult for Britain it had to cut off its lifeline, the Atlantic convoys bringing the supplies.

Although the Arandora Star wasn't actually part of any Atlantic convoy and wouldn't be specifically targeted by the packs of submarines that roamed the cold waters around the British Isles, she would be at risk from a rogue U-boat that would see any British ship as an easy target and another scalp.

But it wasn't just the internees that were nervous, so were the crew of the ship. At the request of the jittery ship's captain hundreds of the Canada bound internees spent the whole day on the deck alongside Jacob and Terry scanning the ocean.

"Three hundred pairs of eyes are better than just a couple!" chuckled the skipper, Captain William Gray, whose jokes masked his genuine fear of the real risk of being attacked, "They're out there," he said quietly to his First Officer, Maurice Colbert, "lurking under the waves waiting for the perfect conditions to sink us."

For Captain Gray and a merchant vessel like the Arandora Star, watching for a U-boat was something of a paper exercise because even if she did see one she couldn't do much about it, she didn't have anti-submarine depth charges, because of her bulk she couldn't out manoeuvre torpedoes and she didn't have a military escort to protect her. The Arandora Star was a sitting duck, and if fate decided that she was spotted by a U-boat, then her end would be certain.

"I've got a bad feeling about this voyage, Number One," said Captain Gray, staring out to sea, "a very bad feeling. We could really do with some bad weather!"

As the ship steamed hopefully onwards in the direction of Canada, the seas were calm like a duck pond, the weather was perfect for sunbathing - warm and sunny - and visibility was about twenty miles. These were perfect hunting conditions for a U-boat attack. Captain Gray would have preferred squally wet weather, choppy seas and a thick sea mist. Then she might have been safe.

Shortly after five pm came the shout everyone had been dreading.

"SUBMARINE!" called a desperate voice, "SUBMARINE! SUBMARINE!"

The tiny outline of a periscope had been seen about a mile away from the Arandora Star by the eagle eyed spotter.

"Where?" shouted a member of the crew, rushing to see who had called out.

"Over there!" pointed the man, "On the left of the ship."

"U-boat off the port side!" hollered the sailor, looking through binoculars and confirming the sighting.

"Start weaving!" ordered Captain Gray, taking the only evasive action available to him.

The order meant that instead of sticking to a straight course his ship would weave from side to side, backwards and forwards trying to make it as difficult as possible for a submarine to aim at them.

The ship started following a zig zag course causing it to roll from side to side, side to side, backwards and forwards, and in no time at all almost everyone on board started to feel very seasick.

Purely by chance, Jacob and Terry were stationed on the right-hand or starboard side of the ship and couldn't see a thing as crowds of men rushed to port to watch the U-boat.

"This is bad, Terry," whispered Jacob to his friend as they both struggled to stay upright, "very bad."

"I know! I feel sick already!"

"Not that!" Snapped Jacob.

"What do you mean then?"

"Shh! Not too loud," Jacob placed his fingers to his lips, "come with me, Terry, quickly!"

Jacob had read and been told enough about U-boats to know what was coming next and he knew that the best place to be was close to or actually in a life boat, because he knew the chances of the Arandora Star staying afloat after it had been hit by a torpedo were not good. And he knew that despite the Captain's best efforts to avoid being hit, he wouldn't be able to avoid a torpedo strike.

Quickly, Jacob and Terry fought against the tide of men who were rushing to watch the submarine and made their way to where some of the life boats were stationed at the back of the ship on the starboard side.

The ship was in total chaos now and no one gave the boys a second glance as they climbed up and into the farthest life boat and pulled life jackets on.

"Brace yourself, Terry," ordered Jacob huddling down in a corner of the boat and crouching down with his hands over his ears.

"Why?" asked Terry.

"Just do it, Terry!" Shouted Jacob, "do it now!"

The periscope stayed above water ominously watching the white whale of a ship which was plodding slowly onwards. This would be an easy sinking for this lethal machine, the U-boat.

At the conn of U-boat U-47 was Lieutenant Commander Günter Prien, a young career submariner who took his job as a submarine commander extremely seriously. Prien, with his blonde hair and handsome face, had film star good looks that wouldn't look out of place in a Hollywood movie.

Regarded as an up and coming star of the German navy, Prien was adored by his faithful crew and highly rated by the Admiralty back home. A superb tactical submarine commander in less than one year Prien's U-47 was responsible for the sinking of sixteen allied ships, including the mighty battleship HMS Royal Oak in October 1939.

"One thousand seven hundred metres and closing," he declared as he watched the ship, his eyes never once leaving the periscope viewer.

As a U-boat commander he was highly trained to be able to judge distances through the lenses of the periscope, "Identify the ship please, Number One?" he asked his Executive Officer or Number One, Sigmund Weiss.

Taking a quick peek through the scope his Number One handed the viewer back before speaking.

"It's British registered, name...the Arandora Star, Sir," replied Weiss, who knew almost every British merchant vessel in existence off by heart.

"What is she and what's she carrying?" Prien wanted to know a little of what he was hunting, it made for better sport and it also eased his conscience that he wasn't shooting the wrong ship. Prien was not the sort of man who knowingly sent innocent civilians to a watery grave.

"She's *was* a cruise ship owned by the Blue Star Line, now she's a general troop carrier and supply vessel, Sir, she's probably going to America to load up and then join a supply convoy for the journey back."

"So she can help wage war on the Fatherland!" declared Prien angrily.

"That's my guess, yes, Sir," replied Weiss.

"Well, my friend I wish to tell her that her plans have just changed!" laughed the Commander confidently, "Arm tubes numbers three and four, Number One!"

"Aye, Sir," replied Weiss, before repeating the order as he did for every one of the orders issued by the Lieutenant Commander, "arm tubes numbers three and four!" He relayed the message to the torpedo room.

Deep in the bowels of the submarine two of the slim Falke electric battery powered underwater missiles were heaved from their rack and lugged across the room with the aid of a complicated system of pulleys and trolleys, hatches were unlocked and opened and the deadly weapons were slid in, ready to be fired.

"Tube numbers three and four ready!" reported the torpedo technician efficiently back to the bridge.

"Tube numbers three and four ready, Sir," reported the Number One to Prien.

"One thousand and three hundred metres, hold her steady, Helm."

"Steady at one thousand three hundred metres, Sir," repeated the Helm.

"She's started jinking, Number One," observed the Commander as he watched the weaving motion of their target! "Steer five degrees port!" he ordered, his eyes still peering out through the periscope, "Now this is going to be fun! This makes it all the more interesting!"

"Five degrees port," repeated the Helm.

"Hold her steady!" called Prien, "Steady."

"Aye, Sir, steady!"

"Prepare to fire, Number One!"

"Aye, Sir, prepare to fire," repeated the Number One.

"FIRE!!" bellowed Prien.

"Aye, Sir, torpedoes away!"

"TORPEDO!" some eagle eyed person shouted from the port side of the Arandora Star.

Spellbound, the mass of internees and crew watched as the torpedo rocketed through the water towards them, leaving a small slip stream in its wake. It was covering the mile or so between the vessels astonishingly quickly. So quickly in fact that nobody had very much time to do anything.

The countdown began.

Ten, everyone was watching curiously as the two torpedoes sped towards them through the water.

Nine, eight, some of the men who were watching started to move away from the side of the ship as it dawned on them what was about to happen.

Seven, six, panic started to spread like fire through the entire group!

Five, four, a riot began as men battled and fought to get as far away as they could from the rapidly closing torpedoes! *Three, two*, it was too little too late, no one could get away in time.

One, a perfect hit! And then another!

The first torpedo hit its mark perfectly, its impact ricocheting through the ship like a huge earthquake, the sound deafening! The second hit less than half a second later with lethal precision.

Deadly and unstoppable, the torpedoes hit the hull of the Arandora Star and kept going and going, ploughing through the ship, first slicing though the outer hull, then breaking the bones of the superstructure of the ship, onwards deeper and deeper they powered, smashing through rooms, destroying engines, fuel stores, propulsion shafts, killing and maiming those in their path.

When the underwater rocket bombs were eventually lodged deep within the pathetically unprepared cruise liner the torpedoes did the most damage! Exploding with unimaginable force, the

Falkes sent the enemy of all mariners, fire, surging through the entire ship.

"GET IN! GET IN!" yelled Jacob, taking charge because he was the only one there who seemed to know what to do, "Come on, come on!" he yelled until his lifeboat was full and could take no more passengers.

"Hit the lever, Terry!" he screamed and Terry quickly responded by yanking the release lever with every last ounce of strength in his body. The lever moved and the lifeboat shot free of her moorings.

"Wait for me!" Just as they were dropping a man leapt off the side of the Arandora Star for their lifeboat. Straining with every sinew, Jacob reached out and just as he was about to disappear under them, caught the man's flailing, outstretched hand.

"HELP ME!" Jacob yelled whilst he struggled to keep hold of the man as the lifeboat dropped from its resting place on the side of the ship and lurched towards the sea, "Quick! Someone! Help me!"

BANG!! BANG!! As they dropped, the torpedoes exploded deep within the great white ship.

For a split second Jacob was losing his grip on the desperate man's hand and he started falling, if the man fell now he would definitely be crushed to death under the smaller boat as it smashed into the water on top of him.

"HELP ME!" yelled Jacob again, desperately, as the man slowly slid away from him.

"Got him!" Terry lunged out and just managed to catch a couple of the man's fingers, crushing them hard.

The man screamed in agony as his fingers painfully dislocated from the rest of his hand. But this was just enough and Terry was able to use his other hand to grasp the man's wrist. From behind them another person reached over and grabbed a forearm, and another leaned over behind Terry and grabbed the other arm. Just a split second before the lifeboat hit the sea the man was pulled to safety.

As the extra passenger was yanked on board Jacob was sent flying, banging hard against hard wood, and lost consciousness for moment.

"Jacob! Jacob!" Terry shouted at his young friend who sat shaking and stunned in the bottom of the boat, "Jake, come on, we need you to tell us how to get away from this thing. Come on, Jake!" Jacob stared ahead not fully hearing Terry's calls.

BANG! BANG! BANG! A chain of explosions were going off throughout the stricken ship, BANG! BANG! BANG! BANG! Parts of the ship, pieces of metal, chains, people were rocketing into the air and crashing down into the water with unimaginable force like bombs dropped from planes. It was like November the fifth and the fourth of July all rolled into one!

Jacob's lifeboat rocked and rolled violently from the force of an erupting volcano of explosions, and everyone in the boat kept their heads down for fear of being hit.

By now other lifeboats were crashing into the sea from the dying cruise liner. But as the port side was being engulfed in raging fires only half the ship's lifeboats were available, so men were leaping overboard in a feeble attempt to escape the flames. Their chances were slim but if they stayed on board they would certainly die a painful death.

Jacob could hear the cries of desperate men echoing through the smoke all around him and he slowly turned to Terry, shaking his head as if waking from a deep sleep.

"Err...we gotta get away from the ship, Terry!" instructed a groggy Jacob, his eyes searching Terry's face as his brain regained its ability to think.

"How, Jacob?" shouted a fellow passenger, "tell us!"

"Get the oars and row, we need to row away from the ship. Row, row, row!"

Three more men were heaved, sopping wet, blood splattered and shivering from the sea as the oars were lowered and the small boat crawled steadily away from the dying Arandora Star.

"Keep rowing!" Jacob yelled as he regained his strength.

Ten long minutes passed and the lifeboat had moved slowly but steadily a safe and healthy distance from its mother ship.

More powerful explosions rocked the ship and with several huge surges of water the majestic bulk of the Arandora Star was slowly disappearing beneath the swirling surface of the icy cold waters of the Atlantic Ocean ready to start her slow descent to the sea bed and her final resting place. No one who heard that noise would ever forget the eerie sound, like the sound of a living creature, a huge magnificent whale slaughtered by the cruel spears of man, breathing its last breath as it let out a blood curdling groan, the Arandora Star gave up her fight for life as her spine snapped completely in two and she slid beneath the waves sinking to her deep, watery grave.

Chapter 42

THE PRIME MINISTER CALLS

On July 15th 1940, after more than two months of endless telephone calls, long begging letters and constant meetings with civil servants, the determined Jane Daniels at the American Embassy finally moved the mountain that was British bureaucracy. She got permission for Professor Carl Becker to fly to the Isle of Man and visit his wife, mother and children in their internment camps.

Jane Daniels had achieved this because Carl Becker had accomplished what many considered was the impossible, he had successfully networked the entire radar system. No matter what links in the chain the Luftwaffe destroyed, as long as there were ten operational radar towers somewhere along the south and east coast of the United Kingdom then Britain's invisible eye would continue to see its enemy approaching from the other side of the English Channel.

Unbeknown to Daniels she had to go right to the top to get the required permission. Right to the very top! To Mr Churchill, the Prime Minister himself.

As Jane sat working at her desk, her telephone rang.

"Hello, the American Embassy, Jane Daniels speaking."

"Call to connect for Miss Jane Daniels," said a formal voice on the other end of the line.

"Yes, hello."

"Good morning, am I speaking to, Miss Daniels, Miss Jane Daniels?" said a strangely familiar voice as she held the telephone close to her ear.

"Yes," she said a little uncertain of what the call could be about.

"Miss Daniels, I am calling about a Professor Carl Becker."

"Professor Becker, oh yes," she replied nervously, still unsure who she was talking to.

"Madam, I have your request to allow Professor Carl Becker to visit his family on the Isle of Man in front of me now."

Whoever it was calling must be very high up in the Government, thought Daniels.

"Oh yes," she replied.

"I have read the report supplied to me by Professor Jim Wilson thoroughly and I have carefully considered your request…"

Oh no, thought Daniels, she knew what was coming next, *he's going to refuse my request.*

"…and I have to agree with Professor Wilson, Professor Becker has certainly given his all to this country's war effort, so I am agreeing to your request, Miss Daniels, I will happily grant your request to let Professor Becker visit his family on the Isle of Man…"

"You will?"

"I most certainly will, Madam, and I will review your request to allow them to be released and return to the United States."

"You will?" *Who is this?* She thought.

"Yes, Madam." The Prime Minister was practising his well-rehearsed lines, lines that he would use over and over again during the coming months and years. "Britain owes a great deal to men like Professor Carl Becker, men who lay down their freedom, their lives for this country, never…has so much been owed to so few…"

"Really?" *No way! It can't be!* In her uncharacteristic excitement Jane Daniels had just interrupted the Prime Minister of the United Kingdom in full flow!

"Yes, really, Madam, my authorisation will be on your desk by nine am sharp tomorrow morning, good day to you."

"Good bye…" replied Jane Daniels but the Prime Minister, Winston Churchill, had already hung up and the line was dead.

It couldn't have been! But the voice was very familiar. Whoever it was, thought Jane Daniels, *he must really be high up in the British Government! No…it can't have been him! Can't have been!*

Chapter 43

CARL BECKER'S DISAPPOINTMENT

As much a prisoner as the rest of his family, for more than two months Carl Becker hadn't left the luxurious confines of Bawdsey Manor. And although he had eaten food exquisitely prepared by a top chef, enjoyed walks each morning around beautiful gardens and by the sea, Carl Becker had constantly felt like he had no freedom.

But Becker had known that he had a very important job to do and he threw himself into that work with every fibre of his being. He had been able to work with a talented team of research scientists and even he had to admit they had made astonishing progress. Now he felt that his work was almost done.

"I'll see you back here in three days, Carl," said Jim Wilson shaking the American's hand as they walked through the grounds towards the boat, "have a safe journey and give my love to Elisabeth."

"I will do Jim...Jim?"

"Yes."

"Do you think we'll be able to go home soon?" Carl asked hopefully.

"Well I do hope so, Carl, your work here is almost complete, just a few loose ends to tie up I think and then I'll send my full report to the Cabinet, I've already sent in the interim report. Jane Daniels said that her request for you to visit the Isle of Man was granted by the Prime Minister himself!"

"By Winston Churchill?" Carl was surprised to say the least.

"I think so but I understand that Miss Daniels didn't realise it was him though!" chuckled Wilson, "Couldn't even tell it was old Winnie!"

"She didn't know she was talking to Winston Churchill?" asked Carl, laughing.

"No, I don't think she did, she just mentioned that he spoke very slowly and said some funny things about the few owing the many or something like that...I can't quite remember."

Just as Carl and Charlotte were about to head for the small boat that was moored at the jetty a sound that no one at Bawdsey had ever heard before bellowed out, sending shivers up Carl Beckers spine. It was the sound of an air raid siren.

"How on earth?" Shouted a stunned Professor Wilson as a lone 109 came into view over the horizon, flying low over the sea, headed straight for them!

"He's flying real low!" Replied Becker taking charge, he started giving orders, "get into the bunkers! NOW!"

"But how did Radar miss him?" Wilson was stood in the middle of the lawn, panic stricken and paralysed with fear staring at the sky.

"Must have flown under it!" Shouted Carl, "no time to worry about that now!"

"But...I don't understand," mumbled Wilson in a trance.

"Get him, get everyone inside, Charlotte!" Carl took off at a sprint towards a solitary unmanned 40 millimetre Bofors anti aircraft gun.

"Yes, Sir, but what about you?" Charlotte was drawn between staying with Carl and making sure everyone else was safe.

"I'm gonna do me a spot of clay pigeon shooting! It's sort of a hobby of mine back home, Charlotte!"

"If you're sure, Sir?"

"Hey! I'll bet you five bucks 1 get him with my first half dozen rounds!" Becker knew the Bofors fired off over 120 rounds a minute with a firing range of over 7000 metres, so he knew he stood a good chance of success if the gun wasn't spotted and if he waited for just the right moment.

"You're on! Come on, Professor," Charlotte quickly ushered the stunned, still mumbling, Professor Wilson away to safety.

As the plane got closer and closer dozens of confused bespectacled academics came out to see what all the fuss was about. They'd never experienced an air raid before and couldn't imagine what hell the plane was about to unleash on their peaceful lives.

"Hey! Hey! Get down in the bunkers, now!" Bellowed Carl, waving his arms wildly, before he got into position and started to take aim, "DO IT NOW!" Obediently everyone ran towards the bunkers.

The 109 obviously didn't know what Bawdsey was, just that it was a large unarmed house on the English coast. He must have got separated from his squadron and was on the lookout to cause as much damage as he could before dashing for home. The Messerschmitt wasn't approaching at anywhere near full speed and so by the time the pilot decided he was going to use his canon to riddle the building with bullets Carl Becker had prepared the Bofors and taken aim.

"Shoot or be shot!" Mumbled Carl as he concentrated.

As the 109 rapidly closed in, the pilot increased his speed to strike.

"Ah! Now you're going to start playing dirty, well two of us can do that!"

Range 1200 metres, estimated Becker, *wait, patience!*

The 109 was closing fast. Really fast! At over 200 miles per hour!

1000 metres, wait.

Range 800 metres, patience, patience!

600!

The 109 was clearly in his sights now and Becker fired off his first range finding volley! His finger gently squeezing the trigger as two lethal 40 millimetre bullets per second fired out of the long canon.

The 109 pilot must have been shocked at the attack because he eased off his attack course for a split second and turned his attention on the gunner.

As cool as anything Carl expertly followed the plane as it now bore down on him without flinching or taking his finger off the trigger. Unrepentant lethal bullets shot out of the huge barrel too fast for a human eye to see.

BOOM!!! The metal bird erupted in a ball of white and yellow flames but still bore down on the gun emplacement. It was coming towards Becker at an even faster speed, a determined ball of fire.

Without thinking Carl didn't release his grip on the trigger. He needed to blow the plane right out the sky to stop it flying towards him and destroying Bawdsey.

BOOM!!! What was left of the aircraft ignited and the dead bird dropped from the sky like a stone.

"Ha! I suppose I owe you five bucks!" Laughed a female voice right next to Becker.

"Charlotte!" Carl turned around, he'd been concentrating so hard he hadn't seen her, "what are you doing here? I thought I gave you an order!"

"I'm your bodyguard, Sir! I can't leave you," replied Smith stubornly, "well, not for long!"

"Charlotte!"

"Will you take an IOU?"

"IOU? For what?"

"For the bet, Sir."

"Oh, sure!" He laughed, then suddenly turned serious, he nodded in the direction of the smouldering wreckage a few hundred metres away in the dunes, "I guess that means all leave is cancelled?"

Chapter 44

JACOB AND TERRY ARE RESCUED

For a long fourteen days the lifeboat from the Arandora Star that contained Jacob Becker, Terry Lowe and another twenty five poor souls, floated aimlessly on the Atlantic currents, heading further and further west across the ocean.

Thankfully, the lifeboat had provisions on board. There was food and drinking water for seven days but because there were seven more people packed into the boat than there should have been everyone had decided to ration the supplies out to give themselves as long as possible to be discovered and rescued. A wooden crate of bread buns, flotsam from the kitchens of the Arandora Star, floated towards them on day ten, and although they were soggy and salty they helped to eke out the meagre rations.

Search, discovery and rescue of any lifeboats from a ship sunk by enemy U-boats was actually very low on the list of priorities of the British government, who were far too busy fighting the Germans to look for any survivors of sunken ships. The chances of being picked up and rescued were very low for Jacob and Terry. In fact there was more chance of finding a needle in a haystack than this lifeboat being rescued.

"How long do you think it'll be Jake, before we get picked up?" asked a weary, hungry and thirsty Terry Lowe dipping his cup into the sea.

"Wait! Don't do that, Terry!" Shouted Jacob.

"What?" Asked Terry looking up.

"You can't drink sea water!" Explained Jacob.

"Why not? It's water isn't it?"

"It'll kill you, Terry, dry you out, I'm being serious!"

"But how long will it be?" Like everyone else on board at first Terry had felt grateful that they had got off the Arandora Star when so many hadn't, but now he was terrified that they might never be rescued.

"Oh, not long now, Terry, it can't be," replied Jacob calming down and staring out aimlessly across the vast, empty ocean. Deep down Jacob had lost hope but he didn't want to let the others know it.

There were miles and miles of vast, empty nothingness on all sides of the small boat and Jacob couldn't imagine who would ever find them in all this space. In fact he couldn't imagine who would actually be looking for them!

But as they chatted something caught Jacob's eye, something sticking out of the water a few hundred metres away, it was glinting in the sunshine. He was sure it hadn't been there a few minutes earlier.

There it was again! Jacob focussed in on it and then his heart sank.

"Oh no!" sighed Jacob, his head dropping.

"What is it, Jake?" asked Terry, "Have you seen something?"

Jacob didn't reply.

"Jacob! What is it?"

"Over there!" nodded Jacob, "look over there!"

"Where?"

"*There!*"

"That? That little shiny thing? What is it?" asked Terry.

"What do you think it is, Terry?" Terry could be so dim sometimes thought Jacob.

"Mmm..." shrugged Terry, "Dunno."

"It's a periscope, fat head!" said one their weary fellow passengers.

"A periscope?" replied Terry, "What? From a submarine?"

"No, from a fire truck," snarled Jacob, finally losing patience, before taking a deep breath and continuing, "yes of course from a submarine, that's where you usually find them!"

"Oh no! They've come back to finish us off!" yelled another passenger.

"Don't worry, they won't waste a torpedo on us," mumbled Jacob shaking his head. Jacob's stomach was aching as if he'd not eaten anything for a month and his throat felt as dry as sandpaper.

"But they might waste some bullets!" continued the same voice, "We might as well swim for it!" He started peeling off his clothes.

"Swim for it?" laughed Jacob, "swim to where?"

"I don't know," said the man, "but it's got to be better than just waiting here to be shot!"

The man suddenly dived into the water and started swimming for his life.

As the rest of the passengers watched the man swim off, they were completely silenced as the waters close to them started to gurgle, rumble and boil like a volcano erupting deep beneath the waves. The periscope slowly disappeared and then a huge thin black tower started rising out of the ocean. More and more of the sleek black submarine surfaced, water washing off its perfectly round hull until the massive metal terror had completely surfaced.

"Hey! That's not a German flag!" called out a lifeboat passenger.

As the submarine closed in on the lifeboat Jacob could quite clearly make out the small stars and stripes flag on the side of the tower.

"Look, Yankee boy!" Shouted Terry, "it's your flag!"

"It's American!" Jacob said quietly, filling with joy and relief, "it's blooming well American!"

A blonde head bobbed out of the top of the tower which seemed about three storeys high and called out to them through cupped hands, "Ahoy there, friends!" It was an American voice.

"Ahoy!" replied Jacob, "Can you come and help us?"

"Hey! Are you Americans?" shouted the confused sailor.

"Yeah, I am, Sir," replied Jacob, "I'm from Concord, Massachusetts."

"Really?" replied the sailor, "Small world ain't it my friend? I'm from Boston!"

"And I'm from Canada!" butted in Terry.

"You are?" replied the sailor, "strange kinda accent ya got there, pal!"

"Don't listen to him! He's not from Canada," said Jacob, tutting and shaking his head, "he's from Skipton in Yorkshire!"

"Oh, right," the sailor's head disappeared and his muffled voice could be heard talking to his Captain, "you won't believe it but we got an American, Sir, some English folk and a weird guy from Skipton, Yorkshyre! OK...will do" The head reappeared, "Captain wants to know what you guys are doing out here in the middle of the ocean?"

"Going to Canada!" yelled Terry.

"You sure are a funny guy!" Called back the sailor, "perhaps your chief could answer."

"It's a long story," shouted Jacob, assuming that he was the chief, "do you mind if we come on board and talk about it, we're kinda cold, wet and hungry out here!"

"Sure thing! Get ready to catch this rope will ya and we'll pull you in. Then we'll send a boat over to catch up with your swimming friend!"

The determined lone swimmer was still slowly ploughing through the water.

"Thanks," replied Jacob, "I think he's going the wrong way anyway."

"Ha ha! He sure is, he's headed for Iceland!" replied the American.

The brand new USS Tautog was a large American Tambor class submarine and compared to life on a small twelve foot by six foot lifeboat it was like moving into a five star luxury hotel for the internees.

Straight away everyone was allowed to have a hot shower and then given clean warm clothes, then they sat down to a hearty meal of stew, followed by pecan pie washed down by tall glasses of milk in the sailors' mess.

After the meal everyone apart from Jacob was allocated bunks and allowed to go and get some rest.

"Excuse me, Sir," said a young sailor, who didn't look that much older than Jacob, "could you come with me please, the Captain would like a word with you."

"With me?" Jacob pointed at himself.

"Yes, Sir."

Jacob followed the boy through a labyrinth of passages, through metal doors that had to be unlocked by turning a huge wheel, and then locked once they were through using a wheel on the other side. They shinned up ladders and through yet more hatches until they reached a small drawn curtain. The boy knocked on the wall beside the curtain.

"Come in," called out a voice from inside.

The sailor drew back the curtain and stepped inside.

"This is the leader of the group of people we rescued, Sir," he declared, standing to attention.

"At ease, Sailor," replied the Captain, "you can leave us alone, come in please," and he beckoned for Jacob to take a seat, "please."

The Captain was tall and seemed to have to continually stoop in the cramped office. He had a thick head of bushy black hair and thick, black beard and moustache. He had an old chewed unlit pipe in his hand.

"Thank you, Sir," replied Jacob politely.

"Now then young man, my name is Captain Wilbur McCloud of the United States Navy, I'm the Commander of this submarine, the USS Tautog, I understand that you are the leader of the group?" The Captain chewed on the old pipe but didn't light it.

"Err, well," stuttered Jacob, "I suppose I must be."

"Well, the others said you were."

"Then I guess I must be."

"I'd like to ask you a few questions if I may?" asked Captain McCloud.

"Sure."

The Captain took a journal out of a drawer, found a clean page and then picked up his pen.

"OK, first of all can you tell me your name, address date of birth?"

"My name is Jacob Becker, Sir, I live at 23 Sunset Drive, Concord, Massachusetts, My date of birth is September 12 1927."

"Excuse me?" The Captain stared at Jacob.

"September 12th 1927," repeated Jacob.

"That's your date of birth young man? September 12th 1927?"

"Yes, Sir."

"Let me get this straight, err...Jacob, so you're telling me that you're not even thirteen yet?"

"No, Sir. Nearly though."

"If you don't mind me saying you're kinda old looking for your age, Sonny" declared the Captain suspiciously.

"Everyone says that," agreed Jacob in all innocence.

"Moving on," the Captain shook his head, "I'm told that the lifeboats came from a ship called the Arandora Star," continued the Captain.

"Yes, Sir, that's right."

"And she was sailing from?" Captain McCloud was making notes in his journal.

"Originally from Liverpool I think, Sir, but my friend and I, Terry Lowe..."

"Another American?"

"No, Terry's from Skipton in Yorkshire."

"Right," said the Captain, "Terry is the..." he looked through more notes, "the wise guy from Yorkshyre?"

"Yeah, he is kinda crazy, and a joker, but a good lad!" replied Jacob.

"Mmm...so you were saying," Captain McCloud was keen to get back to business.

"Me and Terry boarded the ship at Douglas."

"Douglas? On the Isle of Man?"

"Yes, Sir."

"And do you know where the Arandora Star was headed, Jacob?"

"Yes, Sir, Canada, Nova Scotia I think."

"Why Canada?"

"Because we were being taken to new camps in Canada," explained Jacob.

"Camps?" The Captain's eyes narrowed in suspicion.

"Yes, Sir."

"What kind of camps, Jake? Can I call you Jake?"

"Yes, Sir, internment camps, Sir."

"Internment camps?" The captain immediately stopped writing, put his pen down and looked at Jacob, "I don't understand, what kind of internment camps?"

"Camps where they put people who came from Germany."

"But you told me that you came from Concord."

"I do, Sir, but my grossmutti, err sorry, grandmother, Geli Becker, was born in Germany."

"Your gross…"

"Grossmutti is Grandmother in German."

"Right. So let me get this straight, because your grandmother was born in Germany you were sent to an internment camp on the Isle of Man, right?"

"Right."

"And then they were sending you to Canada on the Arandora Star."

"Right."

"But, Jake, you're not even thirteen yet!" The Captain was shocked at what the British had done to the boy in front of him. He'd always thought that the British were reasonable people.

"No one believed I was twelve, Sir, they said I was sixteen, so they wouldn't let me stay with my mom, sister and grossmutti."

"They wouldn't?" The Captain shook his head, "I think I've been underwater in this tin can too long, Jake!"

"No, Sir, they wouldn't."

"Can I ask you, do you have a dad, Jake?"

"Yes, Sir, he's the reason we came back from the States in the first place."

"Go on."

"He's a scientist, he works at MIT."

"Really?"

"Yeah, anyhow he was asked by the British Government to come over to England to work on something really important and top secret."

"And by way of thanks they locked up his wife and family and then shipped his twelve year old son off to Canada for good measure?" replied the Captain sarcastically.

"Well, yeah, I suppose so, Sir."

Chapter 45

THE PHONE CALL

It could have been the call that every parent dreads, news of a loved one in mortal danger, but this call sparked more anger in Carl Becker than grief.

"Call for you!" spoke the telephonist efficiently as Carl picked up the black phone in his office. He was busy tying up any loose ends with his work at Bawdsey before his task was finally finished.

"Thank you. Carl Becker," he announced.

"Professor Becker, it's Jane Daniels," came the familiar soft tones.

"Hello, Miss Daniels," replied Carl, who was on cloud nine at the prospect of finally finishing at Bawdsey, "what can I do for you today?"

"I've got some news about Jacob!" Daniels tone was sombre and Carl instantly picked up on it.

"What is it? What's the matter with him?" panicked Becker.

"No, no, nothing, he's fine, absolutely fine, Sir."

"Oh thank goodness for that!"

"It's just..."

"Just what?" Carl tensed up once again.

"I've got something to tell you, something you're really not going to like. Are you sitting down?"

Chapter 46

FDR

Carl Becker wasn't the only person furious to discover what had happened to a twelve year old American boy whilst his father, a senior American academic had been seconded to the British Government to work on the vital radar networking project. The American President himself was incandescent with rage when he heard the news.

Upon speaking with Carl Becker, the ever resourceful Jane Daniels had decided to send a private and confidential telegram to the White House. Not daring to hope that Franklyn Delaware Roosevelt himself would read the message, she thought that in the very least some pressure would be brought to bear upon the British.

"I just can't believe my eyes!" Raged FDR, as the president was affectionately known, as he sat behind his desk in the Oval Office in the West Wing of the Presidential residence. The President opened a large file and placed the telegram at the top. He briefly thumbed through the pages which he had already thoroughly studied, "just unbelievable!"

"It's true, Sir, every word, I've checked it all out," replied the President's special assistant, Harry Lloyd Hopkins, who was dressed in his customary black suit, white shirt and black tie, "I've spoken with Jane Daniels in London and it's all true. Everything you've read is true. I've also confirmed with Captain McCloud of the USS Tautog that he picked up a Jacob Becker, date of birth September 12 1927 normally resident at 23 Sunset

Drive, Concord, Massachusetts from a lifeboat along with approximately 25 other survivors of the Arandora Star."

"And Jacob is the only American, Harry?"

"Well, another boy claimed he was Canadian but it subsequently came to light he was from Yorkshire in England."

"Well this won't do, Harry," FDR picked up his phone and spoke to his secretary, "Stephanie, get Mr Churchill on the line straight away would you."

"I think his secretary said that he's in meetings today, Sir," replied Stephanie, on the other end of the line.

"Well, tell her to get him out of them! Tell her that this will not wait!"

Chapter 47

LONDONDERRY

It took the USS Tautog three days solid steaming to dock at the large submarine base at Londonderry in the very far northern tip of Northern Ireland.

Jacob shook hands with Captain McCloud before disembarking with the rest of the internees.

"Thank you for picking us up, Captain McCloud," said Jacob, shaking the Captain's outstretched hand.

"Only glad I could help, Jake."

"Will they take us back to the Isle of Man?" he asked. Jacob couldn't bear the thought of returning to the camp and then being put on another boat and going through everything again.

"Well I'm afraid they," the Captain nodded at the rest of the men, "will be making their way back to the island, but I think the Government, our Government that is, have other plans for you. I understand they've already been in touch with your father."

"With Dad!"

"Yes, Jake, and I can tell you, he's not a happy man, not a happy man at all!"

"I'm not in trouble am I?" Jacob panicked.

"Not you, Jake, not you."

This seemed to instantly satisfy Jacob, "and what about Terry?"

"Oh, I think it'll be OK if he stays and keeps you company, after all he's still a child just like you, and he shouldn't have been in any men's camp either."

"Thanks Captain. Terry!" he yelled after his friend, "Wait for me, Terry, wait for me! Terry! Terry! Stop! We're not going with the others!"

Chapter 48

CARL FINDS JACOB'S WHEREABOUTS

It was 7.30 in the morning on the 21st July 1940 and Carl Becker was finishing up at Bawdsey Manor sorting out the loose ends of the radar networking project.

"Carl!" called Jim Wilson from his office, "Can you come into my office? There's a call for you!"

"Who is it?" mouthed Carl Becker as he rushed into Wilson's office, but the Professor just shrugged his shoulders and closed the door as he departed to give Carl some privacy.

"Hello?" said Becker, picking up the phone.

"Professor Becker?" It was a familiar American woman's voice.

"Miss Daniels?"

"Yes."

"Any news on his whereabouts, Miss Daniels?" Carl was hoping that she had news about Jacob, "I've been worried sick."

"Yes, yes, I can imagine, but I've got good news about your son, Professor Becker."

Carl breathed a sigh of relief, "Good news?" He blurted out.

"Yes, great news in fact. He's OK Professor, he's in Londonderry."

"Londonderry? In Ireland?"

"Yes, Sir. The entire story isn't yet completely clear but it seems that Jacob is something of a hero."

"Hero? Jacob?"

"Yes. Evidently he led a group of over twenty men to safety, they got in a lifeboat and managed to get clear of the Arandora Star as she sank."

Carl Becker still couldn't believe his boy had been deported let alone on a ship that was torpedoed!

"And he's OK, Miss Daniels, tell me Jacob's OK?"

"He's fine, really fine, the Captain of the submarine who picked him up, err..." Miss Daniels searched for the facts, "a Captain McCloud sent notification back through US Navy command in Langley, Virginia about Jacob, he told them everything about your son, Sir. They passed the information up the chain, right to the top."

"To the top?"

"Yes Sir, and I hope you don't mind but I took the liberty of contacting the White House about you and your family's situation."

"You did?" After all the delays and let downs Carl couldn't believe that anybody would be interested in what his family had been through, especially not the White House.

"Yes, I did, I hope you don't mind?"

"Mind? No, not at all."

"Apparently, Sir, the President himself has read your file and I understand that he has spoken with Mr Churchill personally."

"Really? The President has spoken to Mr Churchill?"

"Yes, really! And," Miss Daniels was grinning as she spoke, "I have before me a warrant that allows your family to fly back to the States in two days time."

"Fly back?" Carl Becker couldn't believe what he was hearing, "fly back home?"

Transatlantic flights were very unusual in 1940, but the US and British military had developed a safe route which allowed top personnel to fly in aircraft that made the trip by making stops in Ireland, Greenland, and Newfoundland.

"Yes, Sir, so you need to pack your bags real fast, get over to the mainland, up to Yorkshire and onto a flight to the Isle of Man and then over to Londonderry. All your flights connections are waiting for you, Sir!"

Chapter 49

LEAVING BAWDSEY

Carl Becker wasn't sad to be leaving Bawdsey Manor that day and the dreaded boat journey back to Felixstowe seemed a lot shorter than the one two months ago. The academic almost enjoyed the journey!

"I think its jolly good of Winnie to let me come and see your family in the Isle of Man," said the ever jovial Charlotte Smith, who was accompanying Becker, "after all you've said about them I can't wait to meet them."

"You're coming too?" replied Carl, staring at Charlotte. "all the way to the Isle of Man?"

"Absolutely," replied Smith, "you're a very important man, Professor…"

"Please don't call me Professor, Charlotte, Carl will do just fine."

"Sorry, Prof, err, Carl."

"You got it! What were you were saying, Charlotte?"

"Oh yes, Carl," Charlotte grinned, "…the powers that be back in London think that you're so important that you must have a bodyguard at all times."

"And you're my bodyguard?"

Charlotte Smith didn't look very much like Carl's idea of a bodyguard, she was small, she was pretty, she was young and most importantly of all, she was a woman.

"I'm fully trained, Carl," said Smith almost reading Becker's thoughts, "and fully armed," she opened her handbag to reveal a pistol, "and I have used this before! No, Jerry will not get near you with me about!"

For the first time, Carl Becker noticed that Smith's eyes never stayed still for an instant. They were constantly darting around, scanning for any signs of danger. He suddenly realised she was a professional bodyguard.

As the boat docked at Felixstowe, Becker leapt off the boat and tied it up as Smith lifted their luggage off the boat and placed it in the back of the car that they had arrived in.

"Bye, Captain!" Called Carl to the old seaman, "and thanks."

"Good day to you, landlubber!" Grinned the sailor through teeth that were clenched on his unlit pipe.

"Here's a present," Carl lobbed a small pouch of tobacco over to the captain.

"Ah! Thank you, Professor," he replied catching the package expertly, "tha's not a bad un for a landlubber!"

Everything was loaded into the car when Carl turned back to Charlotte.

"We don't need to drive to the station do we?" asked Carl, "It's not far is it?"

"We're not going to the station, Carl," grinned Smith walking around the car and opening the front passenger door for the VIP.

"We're not?" said a worried looking Becker, "I thought we were going straight to the Isle of Man?"

"We are, straight to the Isle of Man."

"I'm sorry, Charlotte," Carl was shaking his head, "I don't understand."

"We're flying! Your friend, good old FDR has arranged one of your American planes to fly us over!"

"Really?"

"Oh absolutely! Nothing but the best for Professor Becker!"

"What?"

"It appears that you are a very important man now, Prof..., err, Carl. So your fellow countrymen are going to fly us straight over to the Isle of Man. I do quite like the uniforms your air men wear..." mused Smith, "they look very smart."

"Read all about it!" Called the newspaper boy as they drove through Felixstowe, "Read all about it! Internee ship, Arandora Star, sunk on its way from Liverpool camps to Canada! Hundreds drown in icy waters! Read all about!"

"Poor souls. But I guess bad news sells newspapers!" Sighed Carl Becker as they sped past the newspaper seller and out of the town.

It took almost four hours to drive to the large, top secret American airbase somewhere in eastern Yorkshire.

After they had driven through the security gate they meandered slowly up to the main office buildings where they were welcomed by an American Air Force General who rushed out and introduced himself as General Gene Wildman.

"Good morning, Professor Becker, my name is General Gene Wildman. I'm the commanding officer here. I'm so pleased to meet you. I've heard such a lot about you."

Becker stared at the hive of military activity that was going on all around them. Cargo flights were landing and taking off every few minutes and although there were no war planes or bombers in sight it certainly looked as if America was well and truly involved with the war.

"I didn't think America was in the war, General," said Becker staring all around.

"We're not, not yet, Professor, and not officially, but like you, many Americans realise that this war is very soon going to be America's war too and we don't want to let our allies down in their hour of need. But on a happier note, I'm pleased to tell you that you'll be flying over to the Isle of Man on that Dakota over there," nodded the General, abruptly changing the subject.

With just two passengers strapped firmly into their seats, the twin propeller Douglas C47 Dakota, the trusty workhorse of the American Air Force, roared into the deep blue summer sky just before one o'clock in the afternoon for its ninety minute journey across the UK and the Irish Sea to the Isle of Man.

"I could get used to this flying business," declared Charlotte, staring down at the patchwork of fields below them, "everything looks so small doesn't it? Like toyland."

"Haven't you flown before?" asked Carl.

"No, never, it's actually quite exciting isn't it?" grinned his bodyguard.

"Not as exciting as seeing your family for the first time in months!" There was bitterness as well as joy in Carl's voice.

When the plane landed at the airfield at Douglas, the capital of the Isle of Man, she was met by two smartly dressed American military policemen, who greeted the Professor and Miss Smith formally before taking them to a large black Cadillac which seemed almost as big as the plane.

Naturally, the large American car drew a lot of attention from locals as it roared along the quiet country roads of the island, through one small sleepy village after another as it followed its route south across the island towards the most south westerly tip and the Rushen Camp.

As the Cadillac drew up at the gates of the camp, two elderly guards bearing rifles that looked like they'd been used in the Crimean War, walked suspiciously up to the car, saluted and beckoned the driver to wind his window down.

"Good afternoon to you, Sir," said the guard, peering into the vehicle, "I'm afraid this is a restricted area and visitors are not allowed. You'll have to turn around and leave."

"We got a VIP in the back, soldier," replied the American driver, refusing to take no for an answer.

"A VIP?" Mused the guard curiously, "can I ask if you have any papers for him, Sir?"

"I sure do!" The American handed over some papers and it took the guard less than five seconds to realise what he was looking at.

"Oh, oh, one moment please, Sir," stuttered the guard disappearing into his hut and made a very hasty telephone call.

"This is the gate," said Arthur Doon, the guard, his hand shaking slightly as he held the telephone, "I need to speak with Dame Joanna urgently."

"Dame Joanna's not free," replied her assistant curtly.

"She will be free when you tell her that there's a VIP in a big American car at the gate and they've got a letter signed by the Prime Minister himself!"

"Signed by Winston Churchill?"

"No!" replied Doon, "Signed by William Pitt the Younger! Yes, by Winston Churchill, the last time I looked he was still our Prime Minister! Now tell her will you!"

After a further two minutes Doon returned to the car and saluted once again before handing back the papers, "Please drive through and up to the Camp Office, Sir, it's straight ahead, the big building with 'Camp Office' written on the wall, you can't miss it, Dame Joanna is waiting for you."

"Thank you, Sir," replied the driver as he roared through in the huge car leaving an open mouthed Arthur Doon covered in dust.

"Ah, Professor Becker," declared Dame Joanna Cruikshank as she rushed out of her office, "How nice to meet you in the flesh at long last."

"Good afternoon, Dame Joanna," Becker climbed out of the car and held out his right hand whilst straightening out his smart suit with his left, "I'd like to thank you for all the help you've given my family, my wife speaks very highly of you."

"Thank you, but you must understand it's a very difficult position I have," explained Dame Joanna as they shook hands warmly, "naturally, many people feel upset and angry to be here but I've always felt that your situation was particularly cruel."

"Thank you, Dame Joanna. I appreciate that."

Chapter 50

THE VISITOR

As Mrs Simpkins boiled eggs for tea, Gertrude and Mrs Schwartzkopf cut and buttered slices of bread, and Elisabeth had her hands in a bucket of cold water scraping new potatoes from Mr Simpkins garden. Sarah and Laila were outside picking strawberries when the large black car pulled up outside the guest house. Since their arrival at the camp neither had seen any cars in the village at all, least of all a huge Cadillac.

"Ugh? That's a funny car," said Laila looking up, her mouth full of delicious strawberries. Mr Simpkins always said it was the worst job they could give the girls because they ate more than they picked. But, because of the long dry summer, 1940 was a bumper year for strawberries on the Isle of Man and no-one bothered about a few missing berries.

"It's an American car," mumbled Sarah suspiciously, her own mouth full of the delicious fruit, red juice seeping down over her chin.

The girls stood watching, shielding there eyes from the sun, as two smart soldiers in strange uniforms got out of the front doors, smiled and said 'Hi' to the girls before opening the back doors. First of all a pretty, young blonde lady got out before rushing around and helping a tall man in a smart grey suit.

"DAD!" yelled Sarah, flying across the garden, scattering bowls, buckets, watering cans, chickens and ducks as she ran, "DAD, DAD!" she screamed at the top of her voice.

211

Sarah was so excited that her feet barely touched the ground as she ran over to her beloved father. When she got within six feet of him she launched herself off the ground and leapt into his open arms. She would have knocked him over had Charlotte Smith not quickly helped steady him.

"Honey!" uttered Carl, tears flowing down his cheeks, "I've missed you so much!"

"I knew you'd come, Dad! I just knew it!"

By this time Laila had run into the house and the news of the arrival had spread through the household like wild fire.

Elisabeth, covered in water and filth and still carrying a potato was sprinting out of the house to join her daughter in a group hug, even Geli covered the distance from her room to the front door in record breaking time.

"Carl! My God, is it you my son? Is it you?" she hadn't dared believe that this day would come.

"It sure is, Mutti, as large as life and twice as ugly!" joked Carl.

"You're not ugly! You're the most beautiful man in the world!" sobbed Elisabeth as she smothered her husband's face with kisses and soil from potato peelings! "You're a real sight for sore eyes!"

"Come on in and meet everyone, Carl," said Elisabeth after ten solid minutes of hugging.

"Oh, first of all, Elisabeth," said Carl turning around, "I've got to introduce you to Miss Charlotte Smith. Charlotte, this is my wife, Elisabeth, my daughter, Sarah, and my mother, Geli."

"Hello, hello, hello," said Charlotte shaking three hands in turn.

"Everyone," joked Carl with a grin on his face, "you might not believe it but Charlotte here is my bodyguard!"

Chapter 51

LEAVING PORT ERIN

"What about Laila?" Sarah sobbed into her Dad's chest as he hugged her and told her they were going to get Jacob and then go home, "What about her Mom? They can't stay here, Dad, they just can't, we can't leave them, and what about Dr Schmidt? What's Dr Schmidt going to do on her own, and who will look after Grossmutti? Dr Schmidt looks after Grossmutti! That's what she does! That's all she does!"

The family were all in Mrs Simpkins drawing room whilst Mrs Simpkins prepared some afternoon tea.

Carl stood and thought about what his daughter had said, he looked up to the ceiling as if praying for some divine inspiration and then back down at his daughter's tear stained face. Then he took a decision, a big decision.

"Mrs Simpkins, can I use your telephone?" he asked.

"Yes, yes of course, dear," replied Mrs Simpkins as she placed a large delicious looking Victoria sandwich cake on the coffee table, "it's so very new I don't even know how to use it!"

"Operator, this is Professor Becker, Carl Becker, yes, yes, the very same," by now Professor Becker was famous on the Isle of Man, and orders had been sent from Downing Street that he was to be treated like royalty, "I'd like to place a call to Mr Hopkins at the White House, yes, yes, *the* White House and *the* Mr Hopkins."

"Tell them, all of them to pack their bags." Carl turned to Sarah as he put down the receiver after the two minute transatlantic call.

Carl was still fuming at the treatment of his family and especially his son by the British, after they'd asked him to come over in the first place! And, he'd discovered that both President Roosevelt and Harry Lloyd Hopkins were equally angry, "they owe us," he muttered, "they really owe us big! They all owe us!"

Elisabeth looked at her husband as Sarah rushed off to tell everyone to pack, "Was that really who I think it was you were talking with?"

"It was, Honey."

"So can we really take them with us?" she asked as the couple hugged tight.

"I can't," replied Carl pulling away from his wife and rummaging around in his jacket pocket, "but this can," he had produced a smart white envelope and passed it to his wife to read.

Elisabeth carefully opened the envelope which had the White House seal on the back and took out the neatly folded paper, she carefully read the letter and looked up at her husband, her mouth wide open.

The note read;

I, Franklin Delaware Roosevelt the 32nd President of the United States of America, hereby authorise an unlimited travel warrant for Professor Carl Becker of MIT and his complete party to travel back to the United States from Europe by way of military aircraft following any route of his choice, from the 23rd July 1940 onwards. This warrant does not expire...

The note was initialled in scrawly, spidery handwriting simply;

FDR

Two extra cars had to be found to take Carl Becker, his wife, Elisabeth, his mother, Geli, his daughter, Sarah, her friend, Laila Levy, and her mother, Gertrude and Dr Schmidt, who still hadn't told anyone but her close friends that she was a vet and not a doctor, to the airport at Douglas.

The party had a flight to catch that would take them home the day after tomorrow but before that they had to fly to Londonderry to find Jacob!

Chapter 52

FAMILY REUNION

It had been over two months since twelve year old Jacob Becker had seen his family, in that time he'd been ripped from his family by the police, escaped, been chased around Liverpool's docks, knocked unconscious, then sent to an internment camp surrounded by high fences topped with barbed wire. He'd witnessed people so terrified and desperate to get away from the internment camps that they risked their lives to get out.

Jacob had been placed on a ship that was due to take him across the Atlantic Ocean all the way to Canada which was then torpedoed. After being luckier than more than five hundred other poor souls who were killed on the Arandora Star, the twelve year old had the courage and quick thinking to escape the flames, explosions and imminent death only to float aimlessly on the ocean for two weeks waiting for a certain, slow lingering demise through starvation.

But someone in heaven must certainly have been watching over Jacob Becker the day that a solitary American submarine had spotted a dot on the horizon and a curious Captain had decided to go and take a closer look. This was the downs and ups of Jacob Becker's war. Jacob had been so terribly unfortunate, no one could deny that but he'd also been really lucky too!

"Jacob!" cried Elisabeth as she held her son in her vice like clutches, there was no way she was going to let him out of her sight for a very long time, "Oh, Jacob, my baby boy, Jacob! How much I've missed you!"

"Mom!" sobbed Jacob, it was the first time Jacob had allowed himself to cry in all the time he'd been apart from his family because, to his way of thinking, crying was a sign of weakness, a sign that he'd let everything get him down and get on top of him. In the camp you had to appear to be tough all the time because the Nazis were quick to pick on people they thought were weak.

"Son!" Carl joined in the hug. He was crying too.

"Dad! Boy, am I pleased to see you!"

Sarah and Geli joined in the hug, Geli being so overcome that she couldn't speak!

"Sis! Grossmutti!" mumbled Jacob as everyone sobbed quietly.

Doctor Schmidt silently ushered, Charlotte, Laila and her mother and Jacob's young friend into another room at the hotel where they were staying.

"I zink we need to give zem some space and some time," she said wisely.

"Good idea," agreed Charlotte.

The small, devoted family stayed in the huddle for quite some time, nobody saying very much, everyone just enjoying being close to one another again.

"Hey! Anyone fancy a spot of dinner?" asked Carl, breaking free from the clutches of everyone else after a while.

"Err...I think I'd rather go for a walk," suggested Elisabeth, "get some fresh air, I think it would be good for the children. They might like to go for a run or something."

Jacob hadn't been treated like a child for a long time. It felt strange but very comforting, a bit like sinking into Dad's comfy old armchair in his study at home in Concord.

"I'd like that," he snuffled.

"Sarah?"

"Yeah, a walk would be nice, Dad."

"Well, let's go for a walk then," said Carl.

Jacob and Sarah ran out of the hotel. As they were all about to set off Carl was stopped by Charlotte, who quietly pushed an envelope into her boss's hand, "it's about Terry's parents," she whispered, "you need to read it straight away."

As Jacob and Sarah ran and ran on the beach, Carl and Elisabeth walked arm in arm behind the children, their eyes never leaving them.

"After all he's been through I'm surprised he's not changed." Carl stared at their children splashing about in the rock pools as they searched for crabs and shells and peered under stones.

"I think Jacob has changed a lot, Carl, he's been through so much and he's not even thirteen yet. It'll take time for him to come to terms with this adventure. It's sure been a long summer! But there's no doubting that our son is a very brave and clever boy."

Chapter 53

TERRY IS RETURNED HOME

Desperate for his new best friend to get the chance of going back to America with them Jacob took it upon himself to invite Terry to go back with them.

"What?" said Terry.

"You can come back to America with us, Terry, I'm going to ask my Dad and see if he can sort it out for you," explained Jacob, "he's sorted it out for Laila."

"Straight up!" replied Terry, grinning, "you'd do that for me?"

Jacob's eyes were filling up again, "we're best mates, Terry! I couldn't have survived this summer without you."

"Mmm...I couldn't have..." Terry rubbed his eyes unable to speak.

"My Dad's sorted it for Laila, Gertrude and Dr Schmidt to come, he'll be able to sort it out for you too."

Just as the boys were speaking, Carl approached them, a big grin on his face.

"What are you two old warriors discussing now?" He chuckled, "opening up a second front against Hitler?"

"Jake could, Professor!" blurted out Terry proudly, "he could open up a second front! And a third and fourth! He's the cleverest person I know!"

"Maybe in a few years, Terry," laughed Carl, "I think he's had quite an eventful summer already, don't you?"

"What're you grinning about, Dad?" Jacob asked, unable to resist smiling too, "and what's that?"

"News, Jacob," he turned to Terry, still smiling, "news about your parents, Terry."

"You *haven't*?" squealed Terry, jumping up and down.

"He has!" laughed Jacob. "He can do anything, my dad!"

"They'll be arriving back home in Skipton even as we speak, Terry," grinned Carl.

Terry was suddenly uncharacteristically quiet, he was never normally lost for words but he was now. He sat down slowly.

"Terry," said Jacob, nudging his friend's arm, "Terry, what's the matter? That was great news! They're safe, so you can come with us now. So? What do you think? Are you coming?"

Terry sat quietly, but eventually he spoke in nothing more than a whisper.

"I can't come, Jake."

"What?"

"I can't come back with you." Terry looked as if he was going to cry again. Until today, Jacob had never seen the robust Terry show much emotion at all, "I can't come with you to America."

"Why not?" Jacob's face fell.

"I can't leave my family, Jacob, they need me now your Dad has got my folks out of that camp in Liverpool, where was it?"

"Huyton," replied Carl.

"Right, Huyton…anyway now they've got a business to rebuild and run."

"Oh." Sadness enveloped Jacob.

Terry grabbed Jacob's shoulders and he looked him square in the eye, "they need me, Jacob."

The boys hugged for a few seconds then broke apart.

"But as soon as this stupid war's over, I want to come over! Can I visit then?" he asked.

"You bet!" Jacob knew that he and Terry Lowe would be friends for the rest of their lives.

Chapter 54

GERTRUDE'S LETTER

Everyone was up early the next morning to allow Terry to fly back to Yorkshire on an American cargo plane, so breakfast was the last meal the group shared together.

"Excuse me, Mrs Levy," said the Hotel Manager who appeared discretely as everyone was just finishing their breakfast.

"Yes," replied Gertrude.

"I have a letter for you, Madam."

"Thank you."

Gertrude and Laila looked at the envelope.

"It's from the Isle of Man!" said Laila.

"Oh no, what if they want us to go back?" Gertrude stared at her daughter.

"Here," said Elisabeth, "let me read it."

Elisabeth calmly opened the envelope only to discover a note and another letter.

"The note is from Dame Joanna," said Elisabeth.

"See, I was right, she's asking for us to come straight back!" panicked Gertrude.

"No, no she's not," Elisabeth shook her head, "she says this letter arrived just after we left and she wanted us to get it straight away."

Elisabeth passed the other letter to Gertrude who recognised the handwriting straight away.

Gertrude drew a sharp breath. "It's Ahren's writing!"

"And it's got an American postmark on it," pointed out Sarah, reading over Gertrude's shoulder.

"Open the letter, Mutti," begged Laila, "please."

Gertrude opened the letter and after a few seconds started translating the letter into English

"Dearest Gertrude, It has taken me six months to finally track you down and now I discover that you're in an internment camp on the Isle of Man, oh poor, poor you! But I heard that you've found our lovely daughter. I expect that this makes up for being in the camp! I hope you and Laila are in good health. They won't let me send money to you, I have tried but they say no. I am working with the American Embassy in London to get you out, a very helpful lady called Miss Daniels is helping me but the British are very worried about German people living in England.

I want to inform you that I am still working for the bank but this time in New York, I had a long journey but it was worth it. Everyone has been so kind here and I've found a lovely house.

I hope you can both join me here very soon, so we can start a new life together.

Your devoted husband,
Ahren"

Gertrude and Laila just held each other and sobbed. They had never even dared to imagine that Ahren was alive let alone fit and well and living and working in New York and now they'd discovered that he'd even found them a new home! Finally, life was starting to look good for the Levy family.

"Goodbye, Terry," said Elisabeth, hugging Terry Lowe.

"See you, Mrs B," replied the jolly Yorkshire lad.

"You make sure you come and visit, do you hear me?"

"You bet!"

Terry turned to Carl.

"Thank you, Sir," he said, "thank you for everything."

"No, it's me who should be thanking you, Terry, for everything you've done! But most of all I want to thank you for looking after my boy!"

"Well, the truth is, Mr Becker, it was Jacob who looked after me most of the time!" admitted Terry laughing and shaking his head, "I'm not normally very good at looking after myself, in fact accidents seem to happen to me all the time! Can't think why."

Jacob was the last to say goodbye to his friend, who he felt he'd known for all of his life, not just two months.

"See ya, Jake, buddy!" grinned Terry.

"Terry, that's the worst American accent I've ever heard!" laughed Jacob.

"Ha ha! That's because it ain't American at all, Jakey boy! It's Canadian! Can't you tell?"

"Nope! See you later Terry, *buddy!*" said Jacob, hugging his best friend, "take care of yourself."

"You bet! Hey, Mr B!" called Terry to Carl.

"Yeah?"

"Keep a close eye on this one! If he were a cat he'd have used up most of his nine lives already!"

"Excuse me, Sir," butted in an airman, "but we need to board now."

"That's for me," declared Terry, pointing to himself, "I like being called 'Sir'!"

"I think he was talking to my Dad, Terry!" Chuckled Jacob.

"Oh, right," mumbled a disappointed Terry Lowe.

"See you later, Terry," said Jacob as his friend picked up his bag and walked towards the Dakota, whose engines were already running.

"See you after the war, Jake!" Terry waved wildly as he disappeared onto the plane.

Jacob watched and waved enthusiastically as the plane thundered along the grass airstrip and up into the summer sky. He waved and waved with both hands until the plane became a dot no bigger than a pin head and then finally disappeared.

Chapter 55

THE BECKERS AND
CO FLY TO THE USA!

The following day the Beckers, the Levys, Doctor Schmidt and the ever present Charlotte Smith boarded a plane that would take them back to America almost via the North Pole.

For four days, the plane hopped across one large expanse of sea after another.

They enjoyed pancakes with sour cream and cakes in Greenland, pancakes with maple syrup in Newfoundland and soon they would eat pancakes with fruit from their own orchard on their arrival back in Concord.

As Carl Becker walked up the drive of their large white house he was met by furious woofing from next door.

"Snowy" He yelled, "Jacob, come and see, we've got a welcoming party!"

"He's been watching out for you every day!" declared Mrs Green, one of their neighbours who had looked after the Becker's dog for them while they were in Europe.

"Snowy! Snowy!" called Jacob and the little Jack Russell ran as fast as its stumpy little legs would carry him up to his master before leaping into his arms.

"That's a nice welcome!" declared Elisabeth, grinning from ear to ear.

"Mom," said Sarah, "do you think I can have a dog of my own now?"

"Sure, Honey, why not!" replied Elisabeth, who turned to look at her son, "It's nice to be home."

"It's so nice to be home!" agreed Jacob.

Chapter 56

A SOLDIER RETURNS HOME

One week after the departure of the Beckers, the Levys and Doctor Schmidt, the Simpkins house felt like a huge empty shell.

As usual, Mrs Simpkins prepared tea for a house full of people, but now there was only the Schwartzkopfs there to enjoy it.

As the two ladies prepared a tea of egg and chips and freshly baked bread there was a firm knock on the door.

"I'll get that," said Lily Schwartzkopf.

She reappeared a few minutes later, barely able to contain her smile.

"Who was that?" asked Mrs Simpkins, not able to conceal her own smile, "and why are you grinning like a Cheshire cat, Lily Schwartzkopf!"

"You've got a visitor," replied Lily.

Mrs Schwartzkopf moved aside and made herself scarce as a young man in uniform appeared in the door way.

"Hello, Mother!" he declared.

"Walter!" Mrs Simpkins flung herself at the young man as he struggled to remain upright! "Is it really you?"

"It is me, as large as life and twice as ugly!" said Walter grinning. "When's tea ready, I'm starving!"

Epilogue

THE BATTLE OF BRITAIN. SUCCESS!

The late summer of 1940 saw one of the most important battles of the Second World War taking place in the skies over southern and south east England.

Night after night the might of the German Air Force took on the outnumbered but brave and determined pilots of the RAF.

Time after time the Luftwaffe targeted the Radar towers and time after time they knocked out part of the network. Yet the system was never completely immobilized and thanks to talented and devoted engineers and technicians Britain was never completely without its secret weapon.

Without Radar, Britain would have lost the Battle of Britain and the RAF would have been decimated. Without the air cover that the brave Spitfire and Hurricane pilots provided, Navy ships in the English Channel would have been sitting ducks for the German bombers and the Navy would have been badly wounded.

Without Radar, by the end of 1940 Germany would have invaded Britain and Adolf Hitler would have set up his British Command Centre at the Brighton Pavilion. Without Radar, Britain would now belong to a mighty German empire!

By Spring, 1941 Britain had changed its policy with regard to alien internment. Many of the people that the authorities decided posed no threat to national security, including Jewish refugees, were released and allowed to return to the mainland and to normal lives. Many joined the British forces and joined the fight for freedom or contributed their skills in some other way to defeat Hitler.

In 1941 The Rushen Camp was still in operation but it became a camp for families, men, women and children, to live together.

The men and women who were interned and who swore an oath of allegiance to Nazi Germany while in the camps, continued getting sizeable monthly allowances from Berlin, but not a single one was released and allowed to go back to Germany before the end of the war.

THE END

Jacob Becker will return in "D day for Jacob Becker"!

Lightning Source UK Ltd.
Milton Keynes UK
UKOW052207050713

213311UK00001B/85/P